THE PIGEON FACTORY

John Richards

with photographs by

Ralph Norris

Cadmus Editions
San Francisco

THE PIGEON FACTORY © 1987 by John J. Richards

Cover photograph and all internal photographs © 1987 By Ralph G. Norris

ACKNOWLEDGEMENTS

Published in part with grant funding from the California Arts Council. Some of these stories have appeared in *Alcatraz* and *Fiction 83*/Exile Press.

All photgraphs are of Detroit scenes, taken 1979-1986

First published in 1987 by:

Cadmus Editions
Box 687
Tiburon
California 94920

Richards, John, 1951-
Norris, Ralph, 1947-
Library of Congress Catalog No. 86-072160
ISBN O-932274-40-4

Next day I boarded a train for Detroit where I'd heard it was easy to get taken on at a lot of little jobs that weren't too hard and were well paid.

–Celine

A Year of Kindness: *Roses*

I spent my first ten years in Roseville, at that time a new suburb of Detroit that grew out of the mud left behind the bulldozers of World War Two. Every house was in the pocket of a pinstriped money-lender. The neighborhood was built of two-by-fours and cheap shingles, frame houses, with a little napkin of lawn out front and half-a-dozen children pressed to the front window of each, itching to float sticks in the ditch.

Roseville. My mother's name is Rose. Rose Marie. And so is my sister's. And the backyard was filled with roses that grew wild and quickly; no amount of insecticide could choke them, and even though dogs in the yard next door chewed at them and twisted the blooms off in their teeth, and though Mother clipped them back whenever they crept too high on the fence, they jumped out of the ground when she wasn't looking: Circus roses, acrobat roses, in Roseville. Ignoring their own coughing and sneezing, their blooms gyrated toward the sun, a transcendant energy that escaped the lethal powder that Mother sprayed on them... and on the trees, tomatoes, onions, zinnias, snowballs and which stuck to my sister and me when we picked the leaves off those plants. Those insuppressible roses! The garden was a forest of roses, a jungle of roses, and everything else cowered in their shadow, those barbarian conqueror roses, red and yellow and white, and even toned back, bloodless with chemical, the white like vampire skin, they burst with life.

In that yard, among the roses with their tense thorns, Mother, her mouth full of clothes pins, flung my father's socks over the clothes line. She hummed a song prickly with activity and the savage bushes kneeled quietly in their beds, listening.

When I see a sky swarming with birds, a curtain of birds turning in unison, my chest swells with flight and purpose. When I see a bird start from a bush, I too take a small leap as if I could run alongside it into the sky, which is partly why living in this city is so unnerving. There are no birds. I did not notice when I first arrived, but like an old friend whom one hasn't seen in months, one day I looked for them, my eyes running hopefully over cornices and electric wires; but, like a strange voice on the telephone who says your friend is dead, I learned there were never birds here. My eyes slid through the blank space on garage roofs and fences where birds should have been, my hand roved over the smooth shells of automobiles that should have been spackled with droppings. I was stunned when the clerk at the hotel said, "Birds? Yeah, I've seen pictures of them. Fella once brought some here, but when they tried to hop into the air, they bumped their heads against the sky and fell down. For a few weeks they sat in the grass; then they died. No," he said, "birds don't take to this sky." Nothing passes through this grey, cinder sky. One sees airplanes here, but they are rare. Their wingtips bend lampposts and knock off hats as the planes roar down our streets a few feet above the pavement. A recent city ordinance requires airplanes to taxi to their destinations, so now pilots are caught in day-to-day traffic like bus drivers. I see them stranded in their cockpits fuming at stoplights and cursing out the window. Children playing catch must roll the ball on the ground to one another. And it's no use inflating a balloon in this city: It bursts as soon as it rubs the sky's rough underside. I see defeated children tugging behind them limp scraps of rubber on strings.

The sky is a harsh ceiling, a slab of living concrete. Storms explode from it with incredible violence, proclaimed in advance by thunderous moans as massive portions of sky grind together. These heavy quakes of air send citizens scrambling for cover. In the prelude to my first skystorm, as the whole city vibrated with groans like those of a gargantuan intestine,

I saw men seek shelter by crashing through store front windows, or climbing into trash bins and sewers, pulling iron caps over their heads. I was bewildered, soon terror-stricken, as huge sections of sky fell around me, an avalanche of grey stone and powder that had me choking for breath as I crawled to safety beneath the bronze belly of a horse in Grand Circus Park. The worst of the storms bury whole neighborhoods, leaving thousands housebound. Rescue crews organized spontaneously in the wake of the storm uncover those caught on the streets (whom they find squirming in sky debris like earthworms turning in sand); bulldozers plow through gigantic boulders of sky that lean against the roof of this house or that. Inside, the timbers ache with the weight of the sky, the ceiling sags, spitting nails into the floor. Survivors crouch under tables praying for the bulldozers to arrive in time, for the sky to draw its dingy breath and rise again above the ground. For one man isolated in a house, the fear of premature entombment was unbearable and he opened his door with an ax and waded out into it; ironically, the sky suddenly reared up and overwhelmed him as the bulldozer that was pushing it rushed to his rescue. With no warning at all, that beast of concrete, the sky, hurls down huge blocks. I saw a young woman racing for a taxi obliterated by a sudden thump of sky, and all that remained of her was a hard monument embedded in the sidewalk and a crimson scrap of sleeve that peeped from under it.

Sometimes a wide slab of sky eases down and nudges the earth like the foot of a bridge. It is not unusual for dogs and rats and squirrels to explore those slabs, sniffing and scratching as they would along an ordinary avenue. Unwary creatures, they follow the gradual incline up into it, grow befuddled and lost. Recently, the edge of a huge slab drifted down in the city zoo; animals stampeded up. I often see vague shapes ambling high above my head, and when I'm riding a glass elevator up the side of a skyscraper, I see elephants and kangaroos milling outside, thirty stories above the pavement, begging to be let in. They snarl and roar and shuffle with desperation, utterly lost. There is no food in the sky, and no trail leads down from it, and the despairing animals gnaw at it, biting and swallowing, until they are bloated with sky and too heavy to be suspended by it, and tigers and koala bears and hippopotami plummet down to splatter on the street below. Even people

12

occasionally wander into the sky; Old folks who have forgotten why they're alive; the feeble-minded, who never knew. I see senile old women drag shopping baskets through the sky; I see empty-eyed cretins pedalling three-wheeled bicycles, singing, pedalling, humming, lost. None of these are seen again until their bodies crash down encased in some broken piece of sky to be identified by remnants of cloth, hair samples, scapulars and tattoos. Lately, for no apparent reason, more respectable citizens have begun walking into the sky, people with everything to lose. My street echoes with the wails of children searching for lost fathers; nephews looking for favorite uncles; stepsons seeking half-brothers. Climbing to the top of telephone poles and electrical towers, they cast nets, hoping to drag loved ones down from the sky; or, perched in treetops, they swing searchlights through the grey, flashing over the underbellies of the porcupines and anteaters that race across the sky, frightened by the sudden burst of light. They form tall human pyramids and the man on top cups his hands over his eyes like a sailor in a crow's nest. In fact, lately I have begun a painstaking scrutiny of sky, because (did I tell you?) my wife went for a stroll a few days ago and was last seen sauntering skyward. I can only suppose she's gone into the sky intentionally, because she, of all people, always had the good sense to know which way is up, and to avoid it. And (did I tell you?) I am searching for her now, and I am writing you from high above the city.

The Tomato Story

My wife's ear had to come off because she had a lump behind it. Luckily, she has enough hair so the hole hardly shows at all. I really don't mind having a deformed wife as long as she keeps her hair over it. I even told her so before she had the operation, night before. "You'll see," I said, "I can live with it. Husband has to expect imperfections. No big deal." I don't know why but that pissed her off.

After she got out, the doctor ordered her a plastic ear, but she said she wouldn't wear it. "It'll be cute, honey," I said, "I never stuck my tongue in a plastic ear before." I was trying to cheer her up.

"You're the one started this," she said.

"What? Started what?"

Far as I could see I didn't start anything. I was just trying to be friendly, you know, everything a husband should be at a time like that.

"You started my goddamn cancer."

"C'mon."

"You started my cancer just like you started every other goddamn thing that's turned to shit."

My wife's grasp of the language. Starts in the gutter and rolls on down the sewer. And imagine, I used to tell her I liked that about her. "It makes you a real person," I used to say, "I like a woman that's real." Now I say, who wants a wife who talks like a locker room.

"You're so fucked," she said.

Maybe I should have let myself be pushed around by her this time. After all, she just lost an ear, and when I reflect on it, I realize that in the scheme of her beauty, she probably attached a lot of significance to having both ears. At the moment, though, all I could think of was I didn't want things to get out of control by accepting a lot of unnecessary blame from her. If I was agreeable, she'd begin thinking I really did cause her cancer and she'd start blaming me for all manner of things I had nothing to do with. That wouldn't help her get over the shock of her operation. It might even cause her a setback. Then her other ear would fall off.

So I said, "Jesus H. Christ," hoping by the tone of my voice to put an end to it right there, put my foot down.

She didn't hear the danger in my voice.

"You did it. You did it and your goddamn meanness."

"What meanness?"

I noticed she was looking at my cigarette. "Because I smoke?" I dropped my cigarette into some left over gravy on my plate. To show good faith.

"You blaming my cigarettes? You saying you got lung cancer of the ear?"

"Shit."

"My scrambled eggs caused your cancer, maybe. You got a lump of cholesterol behind your ear."

She was getting wound up in her face.

"Maybe that doctor jumped the gun. If he'd let that cholesterol lump grow, a chicken would have hatched out and everything would be just fine."

I was enjoying this part. I always got ahead of her with my jokes. I can make fun of anything and I thought I'd win her over with a sense of humor. Why were we fighting anyway? Because she couldn't laugh at what she was stuck with: No ear. It was just a fact. Might as well laugh at it. Once when we were first married we were in bed, she said that's what really turned her on, my sense of humor.

"I thought it was my muscle."

"What muscle?" she said.

"This one."

That made her laugh.

That's why I figured a good joke would snap her out of it now. Stop her from feeling sorry for herself.

"Look at it this way," I said, "Now you don't have to worry about my mother talking your ear off."

That, I thought, was a pretty good one.

Her coffee cup sailed past and broke the Niagara Falls plate hanging on the kitchen wall. She stomped into the bedroom and turned on the TV, loud.

In this situation, what comes next? She stays in the bedroom and watches TV and doesn't even come out to cook dinner. If I let her get away with it, I end up in the front room rumpling the newspaper and eventually get real pissed off and

16

put on one of our Tijuana Brass records that she seems to have fallen out of love with since we first got together. I drive her out of the bedroom with *The Lonely Bull*. Then, we have a knockdown, drag out.

I decided to take things in hand before they went that far. I left the kitchen with a good loud, "Yeah, sure, yeah," and made a big production of pounding my heels down the hallway, walked up to the bedroom door, grabbed the knob, jiggling it like I was going to tear the door off its hinges, and mashed my face in the door jamb. She'd locked the goddamn door. Which was a new one on me.

"All right, all right, that's enough," I shouted. But I couldn't think of anything else so I just stood there listening to Hawkeye make a speech on the tube, and that gave me an idea.

I pounded on the door, and shouted, "Friends, Romans and Dorothy, lend me your ear."

"If you want it, it's on a shelf in the bathroom, you son of a bitch."

That was a good one. Made me laugh. Now she was getting the spirit.

"Next to my teeth, right, hon?" I asked.

I was trying to draw a comparison between false teeth and a false ear, hoping she'd realize everyone has aids to make them look better. That'll cheer her up, I thought. You can see I was doing a lot that day to cheer her up.

"Next to the toilet," she shouted. "Drown yourself."

Something heavy hit the bedroom door and broke. It was a glass ashtray that my father gave me when I was sixteen, the time he caught me lighting up in my room. "Don't burn down the house, asshole," he said as he put a cigarette out in my new ashtray. I'd carried that ashtray around for twenty-five years.

"Nice," I shouted. "Nice going, dear. Good for the door, too."

I should have held back on "dear." I knew it would get to her. We reserved it for special occasions.

Something else hit the door.

"Make you feel better," I said. "Keep it up."

She did.

I was worried. We had a lot of knickknacks, some we bought up North for ten, fifteen bucks.

17

Bang. There goes more money.

"You cocksucker."

I thought about reverse psychology.

"I don't think everyone heard you, dear." I couldn't resist saying it again. "Maybe you should open the windows."

She did.

So much for central air.

She cranked the windows and hollered out, "My husband the conceited bag of puke is a shithead."

That made me whistle; I knew once she hit her stride she'd be inspired. I pounded on the door.

"Dorothy, take a fucking break."

She didn't. She had things to say. I was impressed and I also thought, if I didn't stop this broad pretty soon, we're going to have cops on the front porch.

I ran through the living room and could still hear her at the back window. I looked out the front window and saw Talbot trying to start his lawnmower. Get it started, you son of a bitch. We need cover.

I jumped down the three steps from the kitchen to the landing. The throw rug slipped out from under me so I landed on my ass. Then I was up and out the side door.

Mrs. Hilma was picking tomatoes off the plants along the fence and her kid was standing on the side drive behind her.

I slowed down to a stroll and gestured to my wife. "Got up on the wrong side this morning," I said. My delivery was a little lame, but it made them laugh.

"You don't know what goes on in this house," she shouted.

There are some things of an intimate nature the neighbors shouldn't know. She started to spout one.

The Underwear Story.

Some of Mrs. Hilma's tomatoes had grown through to our side of the fence and she said any tomatoes on our side were ours if we wanted them. I picked a ripe one and heaved it at the window to shut her up. I missed.

"You like that one, eh, Frank? Listen, here's another one."

The Sucking-the-Teeth Story.

I reached over the fence and grabbed Mrs. Hilma's bucket out of her hands. I hit the screen twice, but Dorothy just ducked behind the drapes and kept right on. God, The Sucking-the-Teeth Story. I threw every tomato in the bucket, but she kept shouting.

The aluminum siding looked pretty bad splattered with juice and seeds. Mrs. Hilma squawked when I pitched the bucket. It hit the roof, clattering down. I'm not too good pitching buckets.

Then my wife stopped mid-sentence and let out all her breath and I thought she was going to stop and then she slurped up another lungful and began bellowing The Limp Dick Story.

What can I say? I was cherry back then, and all I had was some advice from my friend, Ralph, who was a fullback in high school.

Jesus Christ, she was telling The Limp Dick Story. The woman was after blood.

I heard Margo laughing a couple doors down, and Dorothy wasn't even to the worst part.

My wife's chrysanthemums were planted along the house and fence. She had so many chrysanthemums I used to call her the Queen of Mums. She had every kind of mums ever invented.

"Okay, Van Gogh," I said. "You asked for it."

I ripped up a huge wad of mums and threw it at her, and another one, and another. Just about every mum she had. I grabbed her American Beauty roses, too, before I remembered they had pickers.

George next door said, "That's the stuff, Frank," laughing his ass off.

But the hell of it was, I kept missing the window. There were mums in the gutter, mums on the side drive, mums in the crabapple, but for the life of me, I couldn't hit that window. She was coming to the part where I came out of the bathroom.

I grabbed the plum tree we just put in and broke it in half, planning to climb in the window and beat her into a coma. It was too green, I couldn't twist it apart.

George called, "Frank," and tossed a couple cucumbers at my feet.

Heavier than soft balls, deadlier than shoes, they hit the screen solid both times. I thought a couple cucumbers zinging down her throat would shut her up. But the screen only dented and my wife kept on.

Threw a bushel of leaves at her. Didn't do anything.

Grabbed a hose, but there wasn't time to turn it on.

I did the one thing I could under the circumstances: I

started to sing.

Mrs. Hilma's bucket was laying on the lawn. I began to keep time with it on the gas meter. Loud as I could, full volume to drown her out, I sang, *All you need is love.*

I waved my free hand *C'mon* at George next door. He was grinning as he opened his fat horsy mouth and his baritone rang out.

All you need is love.

The whole neighborhood was hanging over their fences. I waved at all of them. I missed my calling. I should have been a bandleader. They all joined in, a raggedy laughing chorus while I beat the glass out of the gas meter and flattened Mrs. Hilma's bucket. She was singing, too.

The second time *All you need is love, love* came around, Dorothy stopped shouting. I looked up. She had her hand to her head and her hair pulled back like maybe she wanted to hear us better, like she couldn't believe her ear.

Then she leaned her head against the screen, laughing.

And I kept right on singing.

A Year of Kindness: *Airplanes*

We lived beneath a cloud of airplanes that buzzed over the hot shingles of the neighborhood, the diseased elm leaves. Televisions reached wire feelers up to the planes' bellies which circled just above the tickle of their metal antennae. Father, about to make an emphatic point, his fist raised in prophetic wrath, froze his gesture, stalled his tirade mid-sentence as one of those noisy insects swept over the roof. Plates shook on the wall; palsied, unseen hands rattled Mother's paintings; yellow lampshades, unable to hold the eye of light steady in the failing day, twitched and winked. Mother held her nail file above her finger in glacial stillness. Sister and I, Mother and Father, ensconced in a shuddering mirror, a two-dimensional image of ourselves, the thoughts of each clouded by that swarm of sound, that confusion of pro-pellered air chopped into timeless chaos, drifted into the soli-tude of that paralyzed instant, until the interruption of frenzied racket passed, and Father's fist descended toward the arm of his chair.

The Rouge Hotel

*T*here is a song called, "Detroit Needs Water." One New Year's Eve I heard it on the radio as I sat home alone sipping wine. Those three words comprise all its lyrics, which repeat endlessly as guitar and percussion pound out of control.

Does Detroit need water? I wondered. Even with my primitive notions of Detroit, I knew the city was surrounded by wide natural reservoirs of sewage; that thick clouds of acid fog clung to its suburbs; that the hot ocean on which Detroit was suspended frequently erupted through its concrete streets, scalding pedestrians.

How could Detroit need water when there seemed so many sources? Yet the song was delivered with such conviction that the unlikely phrase haunted me.

What is Detroit? In my mind that night it became a city of scarecrows whose hands couldn't sweat. No water. Whose eyes couldn't trickle sadness or joy. Whose ears were closed with dead skin.

"Detroit Needs Water" inspired in me a vision of black rain falling on the citizens. A black sky washing their bodies with dust. There was no water in Detroit, no way for blood to run in veins, no way for tongues to unglue from mouths...

That song was the beginning of my journey to Detroit, where I discovered a city even stranger than my imaginings.

I crossed into the city on a bus, past vast sinkholes and the massive chimneys that rose from them. Outside the window I saw immense broken statues that towered over buildings. Twisted locomotives rusting in the gravel and weeds beside railroad tracks. Sidewalks criss-crossing in all directions with hell-bent bicyclists in leather jackets tearing down them.

This was Detroit.

I disembarked on a cement platform. A long string of yellow trucks were backed up to it, and a bustling crowd pushed in every direction, walking in and out of semitrailers. Now and then the back gate of a truck was yanked down, locked and the truck would pull out with a blast of exhaust. Another semi would pull into its place. At the back of each yellow semi, a

23

man called to the crowd, "Cab!... Hey you, Cab?... Need a ride?"

Intending to explore the streets, I squeezed my way to the exit stairs, but before I could leave the crowd a policeman barred my way.

"See your papers?" he said.

I handed them to him.

"Out-of-towner," he muttered, nodding to himself. Then considering me, he said, "Mister, I have to insist on you taking a cab. The pavement round the bus station has been breaking up these last few days, and you're not going to know the streets well enough to avoid being swallowed by the cracks. I mean, they bust up real fast and you could get hurt."

He pointed out a cab that could take me to the hotel, I thanked him, walked into the near-empty semi-trailer and found a seat.

The other passengers were spread out evenly, making sure the greatest possible space existed between them and the others. A couple of toughs were slouched into a seat at the front of the semi, near the wall that separated the trailer from the cab. A man back near the gate was reading a newspaper. I craned around to read the headlines he was holding up as if to display them: ELECTIONS CALLED AS MAYOR FLEES CITY... BISHOP DENIES WITCHCRAFT, and so on.

A nervous woman sitting across from me opened her purse and stared into it. As the driver pulled the gate closed, she looked up at me with an expression of immense sadness. "My pigeon is broken," she said, and the instant before the gate locked down, plunging us into total darkness, I glimpsed a pigeon struggling to escape from her purse.

The cab pulled out and as the interior lights began to flicker on and off, I saw the pigeon frantically race across the compartment, smash through the newspaper that, statuelike, the man still held; it brushed my ear with its claw as it flung itself past, and bashed into the wall.

The semi lurched forward, screeched to halts, shouting from the streets was audible, but indecipherable. At last the semi stopped, the back gate was raised, and the driver announced the hotel.

Suitcase in hand, I climbed the front steps to the lobby. With each stair I gained, I had the distinct sensation that the one before had dropped away into a deep hole and disappeared, that I was exactly one foot in front of a widening abyss.

I bunked on the uppermost floor of Detroit's *Rouge Hotel*. When I opened the door to my room, I observed a yellow glass bowl hanging in the center of the room. It brimmed with a turbulent brown fluid. When I flipped the light switch, thousands of cockroaches writhing inside the fixture leapt in panic from the bowl to the floor, scuttling under the bed, under the chair, under the grid of the radiator.

The fountain of cockroaches, their size, some were as large as a bricklayer's thumb, made me hesitate before I crushed the most aged and decrepit with my suitcase. I'd expected the reek of Detroit's sewers, crouched men in doorways, I'd expected soot-pitted glass in every window of every building, opaque and dull, but not this sudden six-legged shower from the ceiling. The door slammed behind me. I sat on the bed, listened to their movement in the wall, behind the tilted picture, their migration in the toe molding. I leaned down and heard their furious running legs in the dark tunnels of the blanket's creases, and felt them faintly rumbling inside the pillow.

Unaccountably overcome with fatigue, too tired to unpack my bag, I threw off my clothes. After a few minutes I drifted into a sleep which I cannot describe other than to say my dreams were filled with confusion like that of a plumber as water rises to his ankles.

The first entry in my journal the following morning is an extended speculation on the nature of oblivion. It begins with incredible enthusiasm, then trails off to nothing.

The next several days were spent primarily in my room, lying on the bed. Immured in a profound and inexplicable lethargy, I found I didn't have the energy to go out into the streets. I would walk down to the lobby door, but somehow lacked the necessary impetus to thrust it open. Instead I dully stared across the street to the brick wall of *Ding Ho's Storage*. The street was always empty of traffic and pedestrians.

Sometimes I attempted sightings from the hotel windows. But the windows of all floors were either frosted glass, or opaque from decades of air-borne soot. All were sealed.

Instead of energetic explorations of Detroit's streets as I'd intended, my attention was slowly absorbed in the complicated microcosm of my residence.

Counting from the first floor, there were seventeen flights of steps in the *Rouge Hotel*. It was an eight story edifice that had not had a facelift in at least forty years. I walked those flights time after time, since the elevator was seldom without an out-of-order sign. Other times, after I pushed the elevator button and listened to the long moan as the car descended, the doors would open to a crowd of bleak-faced passengers, who remained immobile, did not make room for me. Were they lifelike statues, upright corpses? Had not one of them blinked and tugged his earlobe, I would not have known they were alive. Many times the elevator doors parted to reveal a solid wall of cardboard boxes, or over-filled garbage sacks. No attendant anywhere, and once again I was forced to walk. Most often when I pushed the elevator button and shifted from foot to foot impatiently waiting for it, the arm of the floor indicator wildly spinning backward, nothing happened. The elevator simply never arrived.

Finally I did successfully ride the elevator. Its interior was lit by an antique candelabra with three smoke-smudged chimneys each. There was a sombre portrait on the side wall. A small plaque beneath it said that this was the elevator's inventor and his daughter. She held on her lap a minute working replica of the elevator with a tiny model of a man inside it. He was dressed in dark pants and a shirt very much like my own. A slate board and piece of chalk on a string covered the control panel. The note said, "Please write your floor number, then stand in the center of the compartment." I did. Nothing happened. Silence. It was damned irritating, after the long wait and many disappointments attempting the elevator, to have it break down on my maiden voyage. Still: the quiet of the tomb. I stamped my foot, dug my nails into my palms. It continued: the stillness of a catacomb. "Why does everything rotten in the universe happen to me?" I cried, then stepped from the center of the compartment to punch the control panel. The walls shuddered; the candles flickered, then blazed to a tremendous heat; the rug rippled as if a gale blew beneath it; a chorus of lunatic muttering filled my ears; and a thousand pounding hooves stampeded against the outside of the walls, denting them and knocking the portrait to the floor. I fell down, unable to regain my feet until the uproar halted. The door slid open on the dark funnel of my hallway.

My first encounters with hotel employees and fellow residents left me distraught, convinced I'd blundered across obvious social boundaries, or trampled hidden sensitivities. They responded cooly, flippantly, angrily, sadly, sarcastically, mutely and madly, but never casually, and never as if they understood a thing I had to say.

I was never able to spark a conversation with the baggy pants janitor who shuffled from floor to floor with his whisk broom and long-handled dustpan. When I was seated in the lobby, I discovered him kneeling behind the couch, staring at the back of my head. This taciturn man was unshaken by my demands for an explanation, and sauntered off without a word.

The housekeeper, a thick black woman, answered my room requests in a childlike whisper, "Sorry, sir, not today, sir, only got two hands," and if I followed her, she invariably disappeared behind a linen room door.

Sometimes I woke at night and in the depths of the hotel I heard singing, cooing and what fleetingly impressed me as the beating of wings.

In the seventh floor hallway, outside each door, was a straight back chair occupied by a stoic woman, the same image repeated to infinity as in reflected mirrors. As I climbed the stairs past them, they turned to me, all of them, at once.

A substance, a thick soup dribbled from beneath a door. I dipped my index finger into it; it was uncommonly bitter; there were disgusted complaints in the room and violent clanging of pots and pans.

I added my footsteps to the troop of footsteps I continuously heard throughout the building. Who else walked the halls? I seldom met anyone. Once as I stood alone in the hall, footsteps depressed the carpet around me, but there was no one else there. Someone's footsteps walked the hallway without them.

With hours of time on my hands, I learned every nick in every door panel, every gouge in the plaster made by a maid's cart, every crudely broken, badly repaired door jamb. And I soon lost all desire to ever go out into the city.

I memorized all the burned out light bulbs from the second to the fifth floor, and nodded knowingly whenever another one expired.

I crept up stairways in hope of coming across neighbors talking, children playing, couples embracing; but at best, I only saw doors slam shut.

A door marked "Office" had a small, black, cloth-covered window. As I passed it, a sliding panel behind the cloth snapped open. Through the black cloth was the silhouette of a man's head. I felt his breath when he leaned close to the window. "Bless me, Father," he began, "there's nothing I don't regret. I've lived like a monkey."

I was adrift in the *Rouge Hotel*. My suppositions about it always proved inaccurate. Journal entries from this period were recorded at fever pitch, and display an uncharacteristic dread of catastrophe. My urgent interpretations of the difficult events around me are coupled with enigmatic phrases. I was undergoing a personal deterioration of a mysterious sort. I had no concentration. The reasons for this alarming transformation, I believe, circulated in the very air of the hotel. I believe the *Rouge Hotel* (like all Detroit, I wondered?) was poisonously clutched by stagnation; it was a weatherless island in an abandoned sea. When I disembarked there, the ruinous effects of its disconnected phenomena and the stress of no companionship engulfed me.

What in the dilapidated corridors made my reason evaporate, my explanations disintegrate into the dead leaves of my journal? From the first, even as I entered the hotel, there must have been an influence at work that drained my will, sapped me of penetration. Perhaps effects akin to radiation, or white noise were disarming my mind. I don't know. It seems foolish in retrospect to have canceled my schedule, my determination to discover Detroit, but very quickly my project shrank to the narrow runways of the eight floors of the *Rouge Hotel*. I was in the grip of an unnameable bewilderment. I tried to ignore the murmurings behind the doors I passed, but the voices spread through every avenue of my thoughts, a contagion that at once terrified and dulled my senses.

It is impossible to say why I did not leave after that first night or those next confusing days. I had entered an atmosphere of time and space without gravity. It was only later when I was almost completely swallowed by my environment, when it was almost too late, that I was ejected from it by a propitious accident.

I could call all this an extended dementia. I could say I was confined in a rarefied community that resembled an insane asylum without attendants or authority, but it wasn't that. Because for all its mystery, things went along in the *Rouge Hotel* with an amazing sameness from day to day, and although people's actions sometimes were capricious and illogical, nonetheless, they functioned within the undefined requirements of life with a hardiness that surprised me, considering my own accelerating inability to cope. There was an unobtrusive but firm orderliness there. As I sat in the over-stuffed chair in my room and rubbed my bare feet across the wood floor, a vacuum cleaner would tear down the hallway; I heard the maid, a comely dwarf with long fingernails and colorful scarves tied around her head, knock books and pencils and loose coins from a table in the room below. I heard domestic questions settled in mundane dialogues in the lobby; and in the room next to mine, I heard a man clear his throat and expectorate at noon every day, except Sunday. I heard bolts turn, lights flick, keys rattle, and of course, the ever present, but unseeable, pedestrian in the halls. Every day at five p.m., the smell of cooking was so strong that I put on my coat and took the same long, uneventful trek down the seventeen flights of steps to the cafeteria.

I was passive before the confessions of the man in the office, and behaved with the discretion of the Cloth toward him. I walked between the women on the seventh floor as if they were potted plants; when they turned their heads, I pretended I was the sun passing across their sky; I let them drink me without blinking my eyes. I was becoming habitualized to the *Rouge Hotel* and began to wander it without curiosity.

It was then, just before I was entirely absorbed by the hotel, that everything changed.

The *Rouge Hotel* fell into a profound quiet.

I stood in the hallway outside my door, listening, staring at the single bulb hung in the darkness at the end of the hallway.

If I ever despaired it was then in the *Rouge Hotel*, then when my solitude crashed around me, when the innumerable ticks and stutters and groans in the building ceased, and silence hummed in my ears. I ran back into my room. I shouted to the toe molding, tugged the sheets off the bed, to awake movement; I ran down the hallway, knocking, "Anybody

29

home?" and then came back slowly to stand again with folded hands under my chin, and stare at the empty burning of the lightbulb. I returned to my room. I'm alarmed even now as I reread the journal entry that alludes to that silence: aimless sentences wind in circles on the paper, scribbled in gyrating loops, I feel dizzy, as if the words I wrote then were crumbling fingerholds on the cliff I was descending.

When the silence finally ended, when at last the *Rouge Hotel* began to grind back into motion, I was again facing that still canyon, my hallway, with the lightbulb, that solitary beacon, hanging in darkness.

As if in response to my yearning for noise, the walls began to hum with voices and movement. The footsteps in the hallway returned, and I sighed, relieved, but still shaken with a vision of sailing through emptiness, floating through endless consultations of myself with myself. Going in, lying on the bed, I tried to catch hold of my flying thoughts, but as I lay there, I became gradually aware that the voices were no longer voices overheard, no longer simply voices in other rooms which I could indistinctly hear through the walls, but were increasing their volume, competing with each other, as they tried to speak through the layers of doors, walls, and floors, and weave their way through the myriad other voices that separated each from me. I listened to the voices rise, their constantly accelerating speech, until they were hoarse and cracked with the strain. I heard them shout for silence, each demanding the right to speak from the others. "Shut up, I must speak, I must say it." I bent my whole being to understand a single voice in the welter of shouts and yaps and screams, and tried to blend that jumble of mixed-up sound into a single large voice that made sense. The voices rose and fell like the waves of a tremendous sea until the dust on the floor swirled with the vibration, and the paint on the walls cracked. That tumultuous ocean of voices reached for me in a foot-stamping, wall-punching crescendo, and I knew that if I could just reach one person in it, if I could shatter the distance between myself and that one voice in the throng, that my project, almost forgotten, almost aborted with the lassitude of the past weeks, the aimlessness that had reduced it to shambles, that if I could grasp one voice, I would have solved Detroit, and would know at last what it was.

I added my voice to the voices shouting for quiet. I threw myself to the floor and pressed my ear against it, but the floor thundered, and I couldn't comprehend a single word; I pounded the wall, smashed a lamp and in my desperation, ran to the door and threw it open.

There was a man.

And silence.

All the noise and pounding totally ceased.

Seeing him in the hall, I was calm as I had not been before when all went silent. Although he was immobile, I didn't feel alone. He was wearing a trench coat and holding a black fedora over his heart, as if he was standing at a gravesite. He was familiar to me, like a wax figure in a museum, someone you know from photographs but have never spoken with.

I walked past him, to a small table that was lying on its side near the next door down. It had always been there with a vase of red tulips. Now the vase and tulips were scattered over the carpet—the tulips bled into puddles of water because they were made of cheap paper. Why had there been water in the vase? I picked one up from the floor; the bottom of the stem was shaped like a woman's small and delicate foot.

Further down, a part of the wall was burst open; the rip in the wallpaper showed a hole about three inches long that was plugged with a fist. I was fascinated by the jagged skin, the dislocated knuckle. When I touched the fingers with the tips of my own, the fist flashed open like a carnivorous flower and grabbed for me. I withdrew, and the fist closed, was still, would not re-open when I poked it with my key.

I glanced back. The man in the trench coat had not moved; completely motionless, he faced my room.

At the other end of the hallway on the other side of him, were two dark shapes that I had not noticed before.

I almost spoke, but the silence was inviolable. I knew I would receive no answer.

The stairwell door was partially open, held by a hand that appeared to have been arrested in the act of entering the hallway. I pushed the door open the rest of the way. A dark-skinned man, stubbled with beard and with rough features, stood there, curlers in his hair, cleanly shaven legs beneath his skirt. I took the burning cigarette from his finger and put it out on the floor.

The railings on some of the flights of steps were hanging

down, broken in the chaos. I stepped over them on my way to the lobby. There was huddled on the sixth floor with open mouth, a man with an angry face. He held a pencil as if it was a knife. Further on, an old woman sprawled across three steps; she'd pitched forward while applying lipstick. Two men walking side by side, frozen on the third floor steps, blocked my way. I wedged between them, and the tallest toppled several steps down and landed on his back. His ear, torn on the bannister, was hinged by a thin string of skin, but it didn't bleed; he did not cry out.

An old woman registered a couple at the front desk. The man leaned drunkenly against the young woman. Her hand was extended for the key. All motionless, all silent. A frieze of characters stalled in time.

The lobby was a wreck. Chairs overturned, unstuffed, broken. The rug shredded, the threads tripped me as I walked across. The guts of the old wooden radio were strewn over the furniture, tubes broken and crushed.

A man was casually seated in a chair that was upside-down, and the weight of the chair and the man's body depended on his forehead.

The lobby door would not open.

From an active, seething environment, a too active environment that threatened to overwhelm me with a chaos of simultaneous events, the *Rouge Hotel* had become a mausoleum, and I its caretaker. As I slowly walked back through the lobby, I noticed there were old women in masquerade masks, where there had been no one.

By the lobby door, in the vestibule, where I had just stood, now was a tableau of men in business suits.

Four more people were waiting to sign in, but the old woman had not changed positions, had not finished signing in the first couple.

Where did they come from?

Startled now, I ran to the steps, and was surprised to see more people had appeared on them. Someone stood every fourth or fifth step. I was pressed from behind, by a man very close to me, who had not been there before. I looked over his shoulder—the lobby was crowded with people, statues, corpses, whatever they were.

And the stairs in front of me: Everytime I blinked another

person appeared where there had been blank space.

I knew I must get to my room, escape this sea, this multi-plying cast of mannikins.

I hopped between them, frantically climbing the stairs. Every time I turned a corner on the seventeen flights, the next flight of stairs seemed more crowded than the one before. I jammed myself between them, used empty space of two or three steps to build up speed and butt into them.

On the fifth floor, I stumbled into a wall of people who tottered and fell backwards, human dominoes that bore me to my knees, but I threw them aside and climbed over their chests, their faces, planted my feet in their stomachs and groins without regard, climbing to my room.

At the door to the eighth floor I looked back and choked, suffocated with claustrophobia. Every stair behind me had a person on it. Some ascending, others descending. Others paused checking their wristwatch, painting the walls, resting, with their suitcases at their feet. Some with their forearms across their knees, waiting. Stairs with two and three people, all who had perhaps filled those spaces at another time, now appeared unnatural dolls in this bastard dimension, Detroit.

The eighth floor hallway was a solid wall. I couldn't see my door. Confined all around by people, I had nowhere to throw them down. I burrowed, but their legs would not bend. I was caught in a human riot that had gone to sleep, or died, or was not a riot at all, but was something unnamed and awesome.

I beat the back of the man in front of me, I bit his arm, I dug my nails into his coat.

I clawed my way to his shoulders and pulled myself by others' hair, heads, faces, closer to the room, twisted them, used their shirts as grips, dragged myself by their collars. A man appeared, lying on his back, eyes fixed on the ceiling, across the heads in front of me, another barrier was forming of people on top of people. I hauled myself over him, and then dove down, down between shoulders, past sleeves, to the level of hands and inserted the key in the lock.

The door exploded open. Surfing in on the spilled manni-kins, I pitched head first into the room, among my six-legged roommates that were spread over the floor. They disappeared into their hiding places, but I, I stood in my room, horror struck, as unmoving statues of other occupants of the room appeared; men and women hanging clothes in the closet, turning on the lamp, writing at the desk, men in their underwear, the bed crashed under the weight of a dozen couples frozen in the act of love, the backbone of the woman looking under the bed for a lost button crunched with the bone-snapping pressure of humanity.

I backed up, spun around, caught. I had no place to stand. Crawled onto the windowsill. Curled into a ball, knees tight against my throat, strangling me. No breath, no air. As they piled on top of one another, the room now a coffin filling with bodies that broke and tore to fit every space with hands, arms, legs, heads, broken open spilling over me, the pressure of the impassive frozen dead pulled from the distant past, mounting to the ceiling, dark and crushing and pressing me against the window, against the glasscrack

as blew out
the window unconscious or
lost in the terrible hiatus
of memory

Had the journey to Detroit been real or a prolonged hallucination? I believe I was there, in Detroit, and although mystifying, I believe everything I experienced was real. The question of escape does not really trouble me. It happened, as everything else, without a list of reasons offered to me, and so I write it down without reasons, simply as it was. I'm not sure I unraveled any of the mystery of the city. I can't even proclaim the truth or untruth of the song, "Detroit Needs Water." And finally, I can not even say I had been to more than a small corner of Detroit, or that that small corner of the city represented anything but itself.

A Year of Kindness: *Shoe Leather*

*I*n that neighborhood, women dropped babies as often as they baked biscuits. They parted the air in front of them with swollen bellies, filled with restless kicking and fierce unborn mouths. They stretched their hands over themselves astonished at the tumors that grew suddenly from so little beer and fucking. Bent backwards till their spines ached, they labored to contain the squirming life that ruined their waists and made their husbands stray to the end of the sidewalk. From the living room window, the bloated women could see them standing there as if leashed to the house by that strip of concrete, indifferent to the black specks of mosquitos that sucked their necks. Later, the men would swat back the screen door and pitch dungarees on the bedroom floor; they'd lay down beside their wives, sweaty and still on the narrow sliver of bed left for them; the men's strained breathing became rhythmic and settled, and the women, quietly now, probed their distended flesh and stroked it, staring into the half-dark night.

Roseville, city of children, squalling tenacious life that trampled lawns to mud, and paved sidewalks with precious shoe leather. Every shoe was squeezed from a father who knuckled under the powerful hands of a time clock, every shoe was two or three hours of bitterness under the carnal eye of a foreman ... and children, whooping down the street, joyful, wild, tore them to shreds on the rough concrete.

Children scrambled over fences, or alighted on top of them like birds; they flapped their legs over, or perched on the round top of a fence post, shrieking with laughter. The morning air was pierced with their shrill cries that drove dogs to hysterical barking and brought mothers frowning to the kitchen window.

Fathers moved from shift to shift and factory to factory, migrating from one machine to another to make ends meet, while children hurling stones at one another or swinging sticks or falling off bicycles split lips and chipped teeth. The air darkened with smoke as doctor bills mounted. Where's the money going to come from? They worked double shifts, they pumped gas on the corner, they did welding and pipe fitting in their garages; they stole cars and got drunk.

A city of rancid ashtrays.

Smoke thickened on tables and lampshades, a dull brown tar so sticky a spider climbing up from the rug was trapped by it, his seven legs glued to the surface, his eighth waving helplessly until he was batted with a newspaper. Ashes spilled over the lips of tin ashtrays and beer bottles lined the sides of chairs. Crumbs of ash fell down the front of our fathers' shirts, as if their faces were disintegrating into delicate flakes of ghost, as if they were being consumed by worry on their huge chairs. Grey tubes of ash tumbled to the floor, crushed under impatient slippers. Ashes jumped back startled by the bang of a screen door, and flew into the obscurity of the living room rug. My father's hands yellowed with smoke, the nails bent and curled over the ends of the fingers until the nails dug into his palms. His face smudged and darkened. By evening he was a shadow in the corner, a single red eye burning in a twilight of smoke.

Some days all we'd see of our fathers was a pair of legs poked out from under the car, or hunched over the engine, their butts swinging in counter rhythm to a wrench. Car repairs pulled them under the hood, and they struggled with sputtering carburetors that nipped their fingers; they hammered stripped bolts, and bent greasy metal whose purpose even they didn't know. They beat the engine to life dancing back away from it to avoid its shuddering teeth. Whole weeks they'd hang upside down like spiders inside the car hood. A muted scrape of metal and cursing would reach us where we stood on the lawn amazed by that labyrinth of machinery that had swallowed our fathers. A hand would reach out from under a fender, groping for a screwdriver, or grasp the edge of a chrome bumper in a vain effort to keep from falling in and being lost forever. Our fathers would sink into a bed of filthy oil on the engine block, settle into the corrosion on the battery; they'd seal water pumps with a layer of skin. Occasionally, their eyes would flash out at us through strips of grillwork as they journeyed through that cave of sharp metal.

When at last they emerged, we were transfixed with horror at those giants streaked with oil and sweat. They rose up again to their full height, grease stained figures with glaring red knuckles, creases of blood across their chests, staggering in the sunlight, stretching their limbs as if they had just been released from undersized coffins. With a snap of their wrists, they'd fling wrenches and pliers and broken bolts and gauges and wires into a tool box, bang down the lid and grunt at the weight of those ritual instruments.

Their large hands bore the threat of revenge. The air whipped around us as those lethal bludgeons swung past our ears. Ducking like wild creatures, we slipped between blades of grass into the weeds of vacant fields, squeezed through the boards of fallen down houses with "This Property Condemned" signs nailed to their front doors. We burrowed into the ground and hid under branches and sheets of scrap metal and bed springs dragged from the side of railroad tracks. Huddled together, smelling dampness and worms, we'd stain our limbs with mud and stuff twigs in our belts; in our hair, we'd tie nests of dandelions; we'd coat our faces with pine tar and cover them with bits of stone and mulch, press our backs into the dirt walls and rub away the clothing that stood between us and the earth's invitation to quietly and safely root inside it.

Our houses were one story frames, row upon row of twenty by twenty-four foot shacks, the insides tightly packed with dogs and children. Elbows and knees churned through these rooms. They were treacherous passages. Hoovers slammed the toe-molding; newspapers eddied over the floor creating slippery traps; feet flung out from chairs tripped us, and when we hit the floor, straps whistled through the air and stung our thighs. From beneath an end table, ignored or forgotten, we watched our parents pound back and forth. When we outgrew that hiding place, or crawled out from under the davenport, we were banished to the yard. If the weather was foul, or when company came at night, we were sent to the basement, where resided the heart of malevolence, that monster which held the floors and walls together with its huge arms and waited in its cinder block pit for us to descend the wood stairs. The furnace. Its round grey belly was so fat with undigested gas it lay groaning in the middle of the floor.

Hearing the hesitant turn of the doorknob, it would freeze its eight whirling arms against the upstairs floor and wait silently for us to creep down step by step, until we were within its reach. That enormous octopus, a dozen times our size, filled half the basement; its arms, thicker than our chests, reached into the furthest corners. Staring at its iron hatch, a mouth we knew was filled with tongues of fire, we waited, too, floating in its simmering waves of heat. Upstairs, our mothers' uncontrolled laughter, our fathers' grumbling jokes punctuated with "Goddamn," the steady pound of footsteps from the refrigerator to the bottle opener to the living room; downstairs, all quiet, until the furnace wheezed and creaked, a wicked, awkward metallic chuckle, a breaking sound like cartilage in its deep metal joints, then its long relaxed exhalation of cobwebbed breath. It had us. Its furthest limb loosened from the ceiling and dropped to the floor. In one swift curling motion, it sealed our escape by laying a huge tentacle across the foot of the stairs. We retreated behind a broken rocking chair, watching it through the chair's wooden bars. Another of its immense tubular arms dropped in front of us, nudging the rocking chair aside. We scrambled along the cinder wall and dived beneath the workbench into a jagged mess of lead pipe. My sister, crablike, scuttled beneath the stairs, raising chatter there among empty Mason jars. Alerted, the monster pursued her with hot furnace limbs, huffing dust and singeing her pigtails with flicks of its hungry tongue. It licked iron lips, and made a dainty pinching gesture with its arms, preparing to snatch that morsel of human child from the darkness in which it cowered. But in that instant, bouyant with childish courage, we swooped out from beneath the workbench, brandishing pipes and hammers and beat back the furnace, crumpled its tentacles with vigorous smacks until its belly scraped in panicked circles on the floor, and its hollow arms reared away from us. The upstairs door slammed open. Smarting with injury, the furnace reassumed its innocent posture. Mother stormed down the stairs, "I'll teach you to raise Hell in the basement," she said, wading among us with her fists. Raising Hell. Who could deny it? We faced her, filthy with soot and victory.

A Truthful Description

When I tell people what I do, I say it casually, but with a solemn face, standing straight, one hand in my pocket to indicate I am not joking. To myself before the admission, I say, just this once my listener's eyes won't wiggle in his own solemn face, and he won't pound my chest with the flat of his hand, laughing in disbelief.

The peculiarity of what I do makes it difficult to describe with accuracy. In the past I said I stack chairs in the park, which in a sense is accurate, but implies janitorial functions, which is not accurate; others raised their brows and edged away from me. Then I used to say I entertain crowds in the park by stacking chairs, but although this led to suspended judgments of me while curiosity was satisfied, the circus aspects of what I do tended to predominate. Now when asked what I do, I say I look at the world upside-down, so that I can focus attention on the philosophic root of the work; this is the most truthful description I've found.

Every day of the week I leave the office, walk in quick undistracted steps down the six flights to the main floor, turn right, out the door of the building to the curb where a red and yellow tag hangs on a green pole, instructing, BOARD COACH HERE. I get on the 12:10 bus, deposit my coins with a sharp clatter and exchange weather with the driver. If it is raining, he says, It'll be tough today, and if it is shining, he says, A cinch.

At the park I wave at my acquaintances: a Ukranian flower vendor, a retired architect on a park bench, a mad sailor who rhymes sentences and walks on his hands, a bag lady with open sores on her thick, dead legs. Barry, the proprietor of the popcorn cart, pulls his steam whistle when he sees me. I cringe in a friendly display of annoyance, as if my nerves are tender, as if my variety of fear could be that visible. One of these days, I'll blow this whistle when you're up top, he says, and I return, Curses on your popcorn, Barry; May a lawyer chip a tooth on your kernels. We both laugh. When I go down the steps to the edge of the water, a ripple of excitement goes through the crowd that is already gathered there. My regulars shout, Good luck, although behind every face is the expectation, or perhaps hope, this will be my last day.

Unlike a real entertainer, I do no warm-ups, tell no stories, make no speeches beginning with Ladies and Gentlemen; I don't look to see if I have their attention; I'm all business. I fold the grey coat I wear over my flaming red shirt and white pants, and lay it over a nearby tree branch. Sometimes a man from the benches takes the coat from my hand and hangs it for me.

To ensure nothing has been tampered with by a malicious practical joker, I carefully inspect the platform and ladder-back chairs. Two of them are where they should be, and I recover the third from an overweight mother with a scruffy child propped on her lap. I strap my wrist watch to the back of the third chair as I examine it. I put the chairs, one by one on the platform and climb up. The crowd tightens. Newcomers are attracted by the murmers, nervousness, directed attention of others. The second chair stacks immediately on the first chair, and the remaining chair in hand, I cautiously climb up to the second chair. Then I stand the thin legs of the third chair on the upturned, thin legs of the second. As I put it in place I swing up in a daring acrobatic until I'm standing on my hands on the third chair, and my pointed feet are the pinnacle of this trembling tower. I look at the world upside-down, that sea of faces, gaping, pointing, uneasy laughter. For thirty minutes by my watch, as the blood pours into my head and my eyes bulge and ears ring, the hats and coats and bags eddy beneath me: eyes and mouths and concrete. My arms quiver, Look at him, someone shouts, astonished faces, bewildered faces, bored faces, walking closer or turning away, the smell of popcorn. A gaunt alcoholic circulates with his hat out, collecting money for, Da guy up dere . . . money I never see.

For half an hour, seventeen feet above the pavement, I elicit the attention of the curious and indifferent, while I balance in mortal danger of spilling into those faces, that concrete, and through my fear, which I fight as I would a stiff wind or a sudden downpour of rain, the shadow of my father begins to take shape. Blinking away beads of sweat, I concentrate all my efforts on reconstructing him.

I saw my father once a year when my mother let me visit

him in the country. He was a tall, thick man, uncomfortable with his flesh. He nodded through doorways, and chairs groaned beneath him. A shaggy beard and fallen hair ringed his bulbous nose and close set eyes. In those days my father seldom spoke at the table, but leaned over his food and scooped it into his mouth with a clumsy spoon. After dinner, he went into the bedroom with a book and I didn't see him again until morning.

There is a slight breeze, a subtle trembling in my arms.

The tomb is a place of intolerable pain, my father would say, and his wide hand would descend on my shoulder, Here's some advice, Don't bawl when you run...whenever possible keep between the buildings, out of sight... and then he would add, reflectively, It can't be a bad place, even painful, it's quiet.

A mounted policeman stops at the outer edge of the crowd and rests a hand on his pistol. I imagine my own assassination. My knees bend, I am wilting, a nervous jostling below.

I haven't followed his advice, haven't stayed out of sight. Rather I've imitated him, but I've refined his folly to an acceptable sideshow, and I renew my city permit yearly. My father never had a permit, but then he remained out in the country where his solitude, usually undisturbed, was a tolerable eccentricity. He cultivated roses, played the violin on the terrace, and in fine weather sighed at the sunset, the sunrise, and slept through the afternoon.

He might have remained in the country in semi-retirement, and I might have been less unconventional, if my mother had not forbidden my yearly visit. I had no sense till that time my father considered me at all a part of his life. Mother saw me slink into the shrubs once too often away from other playing children. You're too enclosed, she said, Get out of yourself. Her remedy was a round of social pastimes: parties, in my honor, baseball, at my house, cousins, in my basement, Mother, in my closet, searching for books. Above all, she forbade contact with the insidious influence whom I began to resemble with my own gangling limbs and fuzzy chin.

The day my father received the telegram from my mother, he held the scrap of paper in his fingers, smearing the print with his great thumb, while he wiped the back of his hand across his mouth. From the kitchen window he could only see his garden, the short brick wall that surrounded it. He could not see me. When he stood on the terrace, he could only see to the top of the slope in front of the house. A dozen swallows, nested under the eaves, darted in tight circles above his head. He put his heavy greatcoat on, pulled the woolen cap over his ears, strode to the top of the hill, the road, and looked both ways; he still could not see me. He pulled the crumpled paper from his pocket, flattened it, put it back in his pocket and trudged toward town.

My left arm begins to cramp; I adjust my weight.

The station master and the ticket vendor watched him as he stood on the wooden platform of the train station. A strange one, said the station master, Hasn't moved in half an hour. Strange is right, said the vendor, Look at the size of him, and that face. A nose like that's been whacked but good, the vendor said, touching his own nose, I think he's a derelict. Too clean, said the station master. The dark, immovable figure stooped for the brown grip at its feet, and stepped forward when the train rolled in.

In the city station, he excused himself against a nervous, blue-eyed man in grey spats, and disrupted the arrivals gate as he reread the telegram. He grasped the street door in his large hand and violently shook it, then glanced up: Use Other Exit. He had not been in the city for twenty-four years. On the street, a truck jolted in front of him.

The vibration of the heavy engine penetrates deep into the muscles of my back.

My father had expected to step across the street to our apartment, but before him were four streets splayed in different directions, each as anonymous as the spokes of a wheel. He turned his head back and forth, dropped the brown grip to the pavement far below me.

The faces passed his great figure. He listened to them, his mind creating a collage of their voices: he heard one passing couple, God beat me, he didn't..., and another said, Standing in the window...

On the sidewalk, on the automobile roofs, on the wires, on the ledges, fluttering in the sky, pigeons.

I don't know, Henry... Wait for me...The flower girl's shoes.

Perspiration collected on his collar and dripped from the ends of my hair where it hung down. He turned his head from side to side to try to clear it; his neck reddened. Shuffling the brown grip behind him with his foot, he backed to the brick wall, his eyes touching the faces, the mouths that worked up and down.

Now you gotta hear this story . . .

A bedraggled bird looked at him, dismissed him, strutted after a man in a white fedora. His mind drifted among the voices; the scraps of conversation were a silt that collected on his jacket, on his face. He was confused.

One man said, You brought it all on yourself, and touched the elderly woman at his side on the elbow.

Two adolescent boys in the back chant, Fall, fall, fall.

He looked at the telegram one last time, before dropping it, as a bicycle swerved, and a black man stepped from the doorway beside him. The man walked down the street, and my father, preparing to ask for directions, followed him. They had gone two blocks before my father reached to touch the man's sleeve, but a woman stepped between them, and eyed my father's outstretched hand suspiciously. When she moved, the black man had disappeared into the crowd as completely as a drop into a bucket of water.

The two boys leave, thank goodness.

Where am I, mumbled my father, his neck stretched high, looking over the heads of the crowd for the black man, Where should I go from here? He held his hands out from his sides in a tentative gesture, like a man newly blinded. The sweat dripped inside his shirt. My fingers stiff, almost hurting. He realized his grip was behind against the brick wall, but when he turned to retrieve it, he saw he was in a different wheel of streets.

On one visit to the institution, I told my father how I had teetered in a high wind over the crowd, and he had interrupted me with a description of the boy he met after hours wandering the city streets.

He was an honest-faced boy, he said.

A car honks, someone points, I close my eyes.

My father sat on the curb, squeezing a stone between his boots. A dog skirted him, sniffed a fire hydrant. My father did not look up from his shoes. He didn't see the string of pigeons on the iron fence across the street, nor curtains draw closed in the window. He stared at the stone. He revolved it with the soles of his shoes. When a tattered white dungaree stopped beside him, he slowly realized, through his watery peripheral vision, that it was not passing, but was standing still; he closed one of his large hands on the ankle.

The leg tugged, twisted, a voice high above him shouted, Hey, Lay off, Mister, and a moment passed before he raised his eyes and looked in the boy's face.

The low grating of my voice, I concentrate.

Can you tell me where I might find a place to spend the night? my father asked. He knew he couldn't reach me that day. The leg stopped, and my father said, Pardon my awkwardness, but I don't know the city, I'm lost, Can you help me?

The boy's face was clean; hair hung across his forehead. A silver cross lay on his chest. He breathed heavily from his attempt to escape, but when he heard my father's reasonable tone, he smiled, Sure, he said; the pigeons flew from the fence.

They walked grey streets, past cobbled alleys, and between shattered brick walls. When they came to corners, or stepped into traffic, the boy gently guided my father by the elbow. Careful where you go, said the boy, You meet all sorts.

The lights and sounds of the street quickened my father's heart. The hand tightened on his elbow.

Where you come from? asked the boy, but two pigeons between the fenders of parked cars struggled for a crumb.

What brings you to town, asked the boy, but there was a black iron statue across the street.

Wish I had a good beard like yours, said the boy, but a stream of smoke poured from a window.

My father's eyes shifted from object to object, until they caught on the double wooden doors: Hotel. The boy moved in front of him, smiled and held out his hand.

Some guys would say you had to give me something, I hear the boy say, But I helped you from the cleanness of my heart. The silver cross twinkled in the streetlamp. I'm a long way from home getting over here; I live the other way from where you grabbed me. I don't think I can make it back tonight. I'm not asking for bus fare, hell no, but why not spend the night together here, and split up in the morning?

Yes, said my father, shaking the boy's outstretched hand, and they took a room on the fifth floor.

My father once described that night in the hotel's narrow bed, beside the window. Whenever I drifted toward sleep, two huge hands descended and crushed my chest, I jerked awake, finally the traffic in the walls, in the street, the undulating current of faces, and the memory of all my footsteps overcame me. I slept.

A painful twinging crawls up my spine and the faces, some smiling . . .

When he woke in the morning, the boy was gone, as were my father's clothing and money. The boy left only his own ragged white dungarees behind. My father sat on the bed, scratching his beard, waiting for the boy with the honest face to come back. Late in the afternoon, he put on the pants the boy had left, wrapped a towel about his shoulders and went down to the hotel office. The desk clerk's mustache lifted in a sneer as my father walked in, and his stomach roiled with disgust as my father described the boy he'd spent the night with. The manager's head rose over the partition. The men loafing in the lobby lowered their cigarettes. Taken for an idiot pederast, my father was thrown into the street.

They thought they could read the dirt on my face, my father said, the yellow skin, the blood in my eyes.

The pants he wore reached only to his knees. The towel was torn away by the parsimonious and uncharitable manager. His beard, uncombed from the night, was dyed with a trickle of blood from his chin. He was numbed from the tumble to the sidewalk and harangued by voices behind him which seemed to increase in number and volume when he reached the street. Frightened, he trotted to the street corner where newsboys began to tease him. Soon terrified, he started down the street at a full run. Excited people declared a crazy man was loose and pursued him. He was caught trying to crawl beneath a park bench; badly frightened, he was taken to the local police station.

I learned he was put away when I overheard my mother, her laughter climbed near hysteria, describing the dingy hotel, the room he was in, and the tangled metaphors of his speech.

The last time I saw my father was the day I took him to the grave. He dragged his great body along beside me until we reached the hole. The wind made the day fresh, less dreary than the task. We shook hands; he smiled. Why not? he asked, stopping on the third step of the grave.

I don't know, I said, I don't know, the second hand slowly

sweeping, can I, can I stay up . . .

He shrugged.

I've dreaded this day, he said, Perhaps because of what's down there, he jerked a thumb at the hole, But I'll be glad not to have to run those streets anymore. You have no idea how tiresome that is.

He disappeared into the dark hole, I sobbed, but the wind gathers the gasps and wheezing of my effort and scatters them into the crowd where they're lost in the sound of so many feet, clothes ruffling.

It could not be undone; he was dead, gone. He had been a good father.

What do I do? People disbelieve my truthful description. They say, He's a clerk in a small office, shovels parcels over a counter, writes receipts all day. When someone says, How's it today, buddy?, I give him a blank face to his patronizing manner. Balanced on the edge of a chair, twirling a pencil in my fingers, my cheeks still pound with blood, my body quakes with the aftershocks of my exertions.

I'm a large man, after my father; my bulk splits the seams of ordinary trousers. I use the stairs to avoid overcrowding the elevator. What I do is worth any sacrifice. I'm not a clerk drifting among endless days.

I'm not that. I'm high above, thirty minutes a day, at lunch time; the world below is tilted on its side or turned over. Sometimes when I'm near exhaustion, the faces swell, teeth open, and seem to approach, cannibalistic.

Sometimes my father appears on the bridge behind me, a short space away, leans his elbows on the railing.

I twist my head around, a feat that draws gasps from below.

I thought you were dead, I say.

I am, he answers, folding his hands together, and then he repeats the advice he gave me so often when I visited him.

Imagine a violin, he says, and they'll think you're falling. But always come down before you're lost.

He walks away and the high whine of blood sings through my veins. I ease to the pavement, the crowd, and the pigeons that hurry to get out of my way.

On the way back, I don't know the bus driver, and I wouldn't speak to him if I did.

Legs

My wife and I were drifting apart. Financial difficulties, inter-family strife, aggravating neighbors and other irritations were eroding our marriage. Like so many couples, we were on the verge of divorce. I was tired of her voice, her print dress and the dirt from her plants scattered through the house; and for her part, she disliked my stories, my pipe and my sedentary habits. I used to smoke in the room next to her while I sifted the latest batch of newspapers for unusual accidents; she'd bang around in the kitchen or the bathroom, sniffing irritably, as she did her chores.

That afternoon, I was reading an odd story about a man whose personal electrical charge was a hundred and eighty-four volts. Of course he couldn't shake hands with anyone without inflicting harm on them, and so he went through life suspected of bad faith and unfriendliness by others. The man grew despondent and plunged headfirst into a bathtub of tepid water, short-circuiting himself. I was clipping the article out of the newspaper, and my wife was tossing carrots into the juicer in the kitchen (she had an inordinate taste for fresh carrot juice at the time). I pulled the box of unfiled articles from beneath the chair, and was putting the article on top of one I'd found a few days before, about a maid whose finger-nails were four feet long, when I heard a carrot tumble into the sink among the unwashed glasses. God, Blood and Jesus Christ! said my wife. I ignored her, our common manner at the time, and fingered the articles in the box.

It was my habit to reread the unfiled articles before adding another to the box, thereby committing them all to memory. I drew one out that pleased me so much (I had found it months before), that I had not transferred it to the files with the other articles I'd had in the box at the time. Instead I had put it back on the bottom while I accumulated this fresh batch. The story had distinctly religious overtones: it was an eyewitness account of a girl who had a tongue of flame hovering over her head whenever she spoke. She was not allowed to talk in the house, and once, the article said, she had mumbled in her

49

sleep and two dolls and her pet hamster had perished in the conflagration. She was forced by her parents to sleep outdoors behind the house, and died of pneumonia a few months later. The article was written on the occasion of her cremation. I was skimming this article, when there was a loud crash, as if the dish rack, loaded with crystal and china, had been suddenly thrown to the floor, and my wife, repeating her exclamations, shouted a few additional words I choose not to repeat. Again I ignored her. I had reached the part in the article in which the girl's family, Mormon on the one side, Catholic on the other, were fighting over the disposition of the girl's ashes, when my wife desperately cried my name. I started to my feet and dumped the box and its contents all over the floor. I was so surprised I didn't consider the breach such an action was, but rushed into the kitchen.

And I'm delighted I did, for, in that simple action, at the moment my wife's freakishness commenced, our marriage was saved; a new and more loving relationship began. I would go so far as to say, the onslaught of her freakishness was the best thing that ever happened to us.

In the kitchen my wife was lying on her stomach on the floor, like a frog with its legs cut off, in the ruins of our china. She was glaring at me. I traffic in the fantastic, yet I was astonished. I am without recollection as to how I behaved in that instant. The visual impressions flowed in, unsorted, unlabeled. I was unprepared for the strange sight of my wife, that familiar household object, on the floor before me.

Margaret, I said at last, Are you all right?

She was on the palms of her hands, lips trembling, eyes red at the rims; my question was hopelessly inadequate. But as I opened my mouth to speak I found I could deliver nothing more appropriate. Are you all right? I said again, Margaret? She looked so helpless, so beautiful, lying on the floor with her legs a few feet away, against the stove, that I knelt down and gathered her in my arms, set her upright.

My whole life was a preparation for that moment, the moment my wife's legs fell off. Perhaps I had spent years gathering strange stories, collecting and sifting them, with an unconscious prescience that one day my own story would join them. At any rate, we hugged, we cried, I carried her in my arms to

50

the living room couch, and arranged her skirt so that it looked as if she had legs. I thought it made her feel better. When at last I was calm enough to speak, I assured her that life without legs was not impossible, and for once she listened closely. I told her about strange losses, physical deformities, overcome by minor personal adjustments. I told her about the woman whose hands rooted in potting soil whenever she dipped her fingers among her plants, and how the woman mastered her difficulty by wearing rubber gloves. I told her about the adolescent who spit feathers whenever he spoke, but who profited by his oddity with a factory job in which he talked to empty mattress sacks. My wife listened, but was unconsoled, until I told her about the elderly orphan, who, like herself, lost her legs when on a picnic, but who found another pair seven years later that fit perfectly. I was searching my mind for another appropriate anecdote when she uttered the inevitable question, But what are *we* going to do about *this?*

We stared at each other, we hugged, we cried; I strode around the living room with her in my arms, and finally dropped back on the couch. She re-arranged her skirt, and after a moment of catching our breath, we agreed, the first time in years: we'd play it by ear.

I pushed her hair back.

We still have ears, don't we? I joked, but the moment wasn't quite right for humor. Her eyes welled with tears.

Did you have any warning? I asked, changing the subject.

Yes, she said. I began sweating, in the legs. I couldn't help it. I took two baths last night, but you didn't even notice.

She was right, I hadn't noticed. The night before a story of an autopsy had absorbed my attention; a frog and several tadpoles had been found in the left ventricle of the heart of a prominent politician in Argentina.

When I stepped into my skirt this morning, she said, I noticed my left leg didn't behave as it should.

How, I said, Be specific.

Well, she said, It wobbled.

Wobbled?

Yes, she said, It was loose, like a doorknob ready to come off in your hand, or a tooth.

Doorknob, I said.

By ten this morning, she said, It was limp, as if it were drunk or asleep.

Drunk, I said.

Yes, she said, And throughout, it was awkward, like it had had a stroke, or an anesthetic.

Was it like anything else, I asked.

Like nothing else I ever felt.

Her fingers clasped and unclasped my arms; she closed her eyes. She was standing on her torso. Suddenly she threw her arms to her head, saying, What are we going to do? What? Without the balancing stability of legs, she fell sideways, like a punching balloon, and landed hands down on the rug. Seeing her half-off the couch, half-supported on the rug with her hands, a number of stories occurred to me about the small and humorous incidents that often accompany this sort of thing, but the moment was not right to tell them, so I simply helped her up.

Are you in pain? I asked.

No, she said.

Can I get you a glass of water?

What does that have to do with anything? she asked, and a smile flickered across her face, Yes, yes, she said, I would like something. A glass of carrot juice, perhaps.

I took several carrots from the refrigerator, set them on the counter top, before I realized the sink was already scattered with carrots, that I was completing what my wife had begun a few minutes before when she had been whole. My hand shook badly, I overturned a glass as I lifted a fallen carrot from the sink and washed it under the faucet. There was a sound behind me. I thought my wife had followed me into the kitchen seeking the comfort of our shared presence, but I could not turn around, could not bear to see her swinging in on her hands, looking up at me. I'll bring it to you, dear, I said softly, Please just sit down and I'll bring it to you. Another slight shuffling sound, a sound, I thought of her hands slapping the linoleum. My throat tightened. Really, love, I said, I'll be in in a moment, rest ... What? my wife called from the other room. Just a mo ..., I stopped short, I turned and nearly dropped my carrots. I could not have been more shocked than the obstetrician who assisted as a woman gave birth to forty black widow spiders, or the nurse's aid who saw an angel-faced paraplegic grow wings and escape from a convalescent home (only to be shot down over a forest by a poacher). My wife's legs, still attached to one another, were struggling to their feet by the stove. The right foot was patting around, flopping forward and back, like the foreleg of an insect. I couldn't take my eyes from the toes; painted red, they seemed absurd, and threatening. The big toe twisted up and down. The feet flattened on the floor, and all at once, the legs bounced upright, stood bodiless in front of me, my wife's shapely legs stood in front of me, and started hopping up and down on the balls of their feet. Without the weight of the body on them, they hopped nearly to the ceiling. I staggered, carrots in hand, into the living room.

Carrot juice, my wife laughed, not carrots.

I was speechless. In a futile protective gesture, I stood between her and the kitchen, but the legs bounced into the room, light as feathers across the overstuffed chair, leaping, spinning, turning, displaying a freedom and agility properly attached legs never have. My wife gaped, her eyes widened, she was bewildered, confused, a glint of madness flickered across her face as the legs came to a jogging halt before her, pumping up and down in place.

Shall I describe those moments?

My wife beckoned to the legs, to stroke them, but they danced out of reach; I grew impatient and attempted to tackle them, but they eluded me; yet, they seemed to insist that we accept them. Accept them as what? I wondered. They danced in the midst of our despair. How inventive they were! They did somersault tricks, slapstick imitations of splits and softshoe. Before long we were laughing and clapping our hands together, and the legs leaped into the air, and touched heels together.

When the novelty had worn off, after a few hours, I had a sudden realization.

Blood, I said, pointing to the legs.

Following my gaze, my wife said, Don't be upset, dear. Don't swear at them.

Blood, I cried, There's no blood!

The legs were smooth flesh across the top where they were attached to each other: no blood or gore, no obtruding organs, no gaping wound, torn flesh nor abrasions, no bruises, cuts nor phlegmy residue, nothing but creamy flesh across the top, the same supple consistency of the thighs. I reached to touch them, but the legs, still suspicious of me, jumped out of reach. I grew excited. It was a discovery. If I could not examine the legs I could at least examine my wife, and my attention turned to her. She pushed the cushions with her hands attempting to back away from me. Before she had moved more than an inch, I had her skirt hoisted over her face and was studying the damage: there was none! Her crevices were precisely where they should have been, in perfect condition, that is, as far as an eyeball inspection could ascertain, and she was perfectly healed all around her body. Smooth fleshy muscles across her bottom. Her butt swept beneath her in lovely handfuls of flesh. I ran my fingers over her.

How does that feel? I asked.

She put the skirt down, watched me watching her. She was as curious as I. She looked surprised.

Why, she said, That feels good.

An aspect of our married life, which we thought dead, we discovered had been lying dormant, and it now sprang to life during my tactile experiments in this strange terrain. We ignored the legs, which frantically hopped and kicked. I suppose we assumed they were included in the events transpiring between us. But the legs felt differently; my wife's delicate foot, and flaming red toenail, struck my behind at a crucial moment and the natural course of events was interrupted, only to be resumed a few minutes later, in the appropriate room of the house. I rode my wife piggy-back to the bedroom, we closed the door, and while the legs kicked wildly outside, we dispersed, in the next few hours, the last trace of marital discord.

My wife adjusted quickly to leglessness. Her arms developed surprising strength, and we rigged a series of poles and ropes through the house that she used to swing from room to room. The vigorous exercise rehabilitated her physique, her belly flattened, her breasts tightened, her back, in fact, broadened; the creeping flabbiness disappeared. Sometimes as we sat at the table, she and I, the legs jogging in place nearby, I would be suddenly stunned by her extraordinary beauty.

She'd smile.

The months that followed passed in a happy rush. The three

of us living together, a small closely knit family. The first weeks we never went out. I shopped, banked, paid bills, hurried home to be with them.

The outside world was a laugh we had in our conspiracy against it. We grew adventuresome; I pulled the car into the garage, my wife climbed in, the legs hid under the blanket in the back seat, and we drove through the suburbs. The plain houses and bland faces we saw out there, how funny it all seemed. My wife and I held hands, and the legs tapped happily in the back seat. Having carefully prepared our friends on the telephone, we invited them to visit. The bliss of our existence communicated to them more fully than our explanations. Many evenings, as we all sat around the living room, entertained by the legs, a husband or wife would look wistfully at their own spouse's limbs.

The legs—how they changed from tyrant child, from temper tantrums when they sensed even the slightest hint of exclusion, into a trusting pair of legs which met us in the hallway when we rose in the morning, displaying for our pleasure their newest tricks: childish variations of spins and leaps, and we, the parents, took immense pride in each new activity.

And I've changed. I've thrown out my files. No longer collect articles. Even that dusty old closet, my memory, I expect to find, one day soon, wiped clean.

Are there any drawbacks at all to this new life? Perhaps one. I do, occasionally, resent the aggressive intrusions of the journalists who hide in our shrubbery, but this distraction is easily circumvented by turning on the sprinklers.

A Year of Kindness: *Landlords*
(For Naomi Schwartz)

I'm sorry to hear about your house. I know the feeling of homelessness, what it is to shuffle possessions into boxes and to leave a place that is safe and familiar, but that does you no good. There's no relief for no place to go, only another place, and that only when you've been there a year or two. The size of the rooms in your own house fits the shape of your body. It's true that the way you think is formed by the way the space you inhabit is cut up, arranged. What do I know? There is loss with every move. Valued objects are not only broken, but they disappear out of the boxes they are packed in. It's the damnedest thing you can imagine. A magician's trick. They are in one place, and you keep an eye on them, but when you get around to unpacking them, to put them on an unfamiliar mantle, or windowsill, they are gone. When you hold them in your hands, they are suddenly nothing more than gravel and twigs. Perhaps I am making too much of your eviction notice. I've had evictions, been told to leave, both politely, and not so politely. It is all death, the end. And from the end you have to direct yourself into a new space from which you build to what you had, or to something better, and all the time you must fight the fatigue, the giving up. I don't know if I am making sense at all. My own bedroom is stacked from floor to ceiling with cardboard boxes, and this apartment which was my enemy a year ago, with all its damned nuisances, is now my refuge. I know just how far I can walk in every room; I admit only who I want to admit; the arrangement of the furniture resembles my personality; and my friends are now familiar with me in this place: it is a language I don't have to speak with them. Now there is this dark spot, this dark wall of boxes, that are advancing through the night, filling my dreams with the awful smell of cardboard.

I was once stranded on the freeway in California, facing a three or four day hitch back to Michigan I had not expected. That was the loneliest I have ever felt, sitting on my pack with my thumb out, and it was homelessness, or the inaccessibility of home that I felt, the utter disconnect my body was from all the other bodies in the world, I felt utterly vulnerable, suddenly the thinness of my skin, the shell of my skull, the dirt eating through the thread of my jeans, the pack with its meager provisions, and the ten or fifteen dollars I had in my pocket. I was thrown out, thrown down, and I could have disappeared in the weeds next to the pavement, and no one would have found me. I wouldn't have been the first to re-enter the earth through an unmarked passage, but nothing would have dug in the offal, not an animal would have sniffed me. There were no animals there, only the rubber singing past, the hot metal, the cement. Drivers averted their eyes, embarrassed by the look of me.

There can be hope when you move. The labor of moving eats it up. When you see your blankets laying on the cement, or see your dishes tumbled in boxes, you cringe. The "Fragile" you've written on the side of the box is a pointless gesture; it is impossible to do any more than throw things atop one another, and drive as fast as you can toward you know not what, hurry to get someplace where you can unpack and assess the damage, glue the china, put the handles back on the cups, shake the curtains out and wash them, again, replace the glass on the drawings, and examine them to see how badly they've been scratched this time. Every time my wife and I have moved, we have lost something, a suitcase, a typewriter, a drawing, a bowl, always something.

If it rains when you carry your possessions down to the street, when your couch is in the back of the pickup, you will have to live with the rain stink that gets in it, or, if it is dry outside, you'll never get all the dust out of the fabric. The dust is different than accumulates over the years, it's not mixed with friendship and casual use. The couch is dumped against the side of the truck bed, and is streaked from the metal railing. Worse than the dirt are the scratches and tears when you pack a table against the couch, or shove a trunk against its end. Often there is nothing so obvious as a rip in the upholstery, which you could repair, or at least keep children's fingers from, but the cloth is stressed, uneven stretches that you don't notice, but which indicate delapidation, wearing away. As if the furniture or dishes or blankets were alive, the movement has an upsetting effect, they just aren't as good after they've been moved, they don't have the same freshness, they are a little dirtier, a little more ruddy complexioned, scarred, scabbed, as if moving were a near fatal bout of illness.

The landlord is always a nice guy when the rent is on time, when he doesn't have to fix the toilet. Never forget you're his profit, you're his way of making a buck, and when something else becomes more profitable, then you're out. Evictions make you understand where you are in the pyramid, how the universe regards you. Landlords are usually little guys too, but they own the building, they wear the captain's hat, they are boss, little guys with big, if narrowly conceived notions of who they are—they are the difference between fantasy and imagination.

I fear I will once again sit on milk crates, as I have at other times, at other places, that everything I own, if I continue to own anything, will be in storage in some other city, and I will be on bare wooden floors, in an apartment with sheets hung over the windows, and paint chipped throughout, and a landlord who comes in twice a week with a bucket and an eight inch paint brush, to spread poison around the woodwork, up the wall, to kill the cockroaches.

My wife and I are trying to make it for a few months more. We have been desperate and at each other's throats. Her fingers tap the arm of the chair, her foot goes up and down, I get singing and dancing, all desperate, try to cover it, we bicker, because there is no place for us, no money. There is only this place we cannot afford, there are only other places down the road, which already have too many applicants, which are too expensive for us, there is nothing, while we try to talk our talent and imaginations back into being, but they are buried under the need for new shoes, for a night out, for a school system and a neighborhood for our daughter. There is only worry, and we take turns each night staying awake with it, nursing it, talking to it, it hunched at the edge of the bed, its thin fingers slipping under the covers and touching a warm thigh now and again, at the moment of sleep, whispering, "Where to live, what to do, you thought you were good, well, look at you now."

Foolish me. I haven't yet given up. Sometimes I feel like the man accused of witchcraft who would not confess, so they took him out back of the Salem jail and laid a door on him, and stacked the door with rocks, and when they leaned down to hear his confession, they heard him whisper, "More weight."

I'm sorry you have to move and don't want to. I hope you've found another place and it's better than the one you've been in, so you can thumb your nose at your former landlord, at least for the time being, until the next time, when your landlord takes a dislike to the way you walk his sidewalk, or the company you keep.

We are here for the time being. We don't know for how long. Maybe days, maybe months, maybe years. We don't know how we're going to make the rent wherever we go. We will or we won't.

You're moving. I know, I know, I hate it.

The Fall of Detroit
(And the Last Days of Toledo, Ohio)

*T*he first refugees arrived on foot, carrying a few of their belongings in their hands. It was late, but the mayor, standing on the porch in his nightshirt, granted special permission for them to enter the city. A cordon of police directed them to a school where they were to be housed until morning and decisions could be made as to what to do with them.

The Red Cross brought a truckload of blankets and mattresses. This first group, about a hundred and fifty men, women and children, all wore shocked looks on their faces. Some were in rags, some in business suits, some sat quietly with their wives holding hands and comforting infants, others wept and fainted, or cried out.

It was impossible for us to know that by morning there would be thousands more.

In fact, hundreds more appeared within the hour. When they were spotted about a mile off the city limit, a runner from the suburbs was sent to us. The first vehicle, a yellow semi filled to the brim with refugees, rolled slowly toward the city on a dozen flat tires. At the last crossroads before entering town, the driver slumped over the wheel and the vehicle crept off the highway and overturned. People hanging on the side were crushed. Others were trampled as passengers attempted to clamber from the windows on the other side.

Scores of people followed behind the bus. All were directed to the school. The school building quickly filled, its classrooms and hallways lined with people, so the new arrivals stayed outside in the school yard. They were given sleeping gear. It was a warm night and clear with no danger of rain.

Some citizens voiced their concern that perhaps we should not open our gates until we knew more about the crisis, but with the gravel voice of authority, the mayor declared into a bull-horn, "They're people just like us, even if they are from Detroit," his chest swelled with a serious breath. "We've got to help." He invoked his emergency powers and called more

65

police into service.

Even during these early hours, there was almost no control. Refugees entered the city by several routes, dispersing in the city parks and making their beds on the steps of public buildings. Some citizens were surprised to see friends turn up among them and invited them into their homes. The railway station and airport bristled with refugees from unscheduled locomotives and airplanes.

Their numbers swelled steadily and inexorably. They walked out of the corn fields surrounding the city, climbed from makeshift rafts in the dirty river. They seemed to drop like leaves from the trees around us. An endless flow on foot, a few on roller skates and others, just barely breathing, were dragged past the flashing blue police lights.

Rumors of an epidemic sprung up among guards and other officials, which sent representatives of the city council to my door, banging with their fists and waking the whole household and the neighborhood.

"Doctor, they're dying like flies in Detroit!"

"The streets are flooded with corpses!"

"Disease coats their clothes, we need you!"

A dozen men milled around my vestibule, each with frantic exclamations bursting from his lips. I nodded to them, gathered my instruments, trying to gain time to sort out the confusion.

The streets were already lined with people as we raced through them. The sirens and lights of emergency vehicles alerted the citizenry and they came out of their houses with puzzled looks on their faces, mingling with the refugees who stumbled and bumped into them.

Brilliant spotlights shone down on the school yard drenching the hundreds of refugees there in an unearthly white light. Red Cross officials circulated among them, sorting out the casualties and trying, at the same time, to gather names. The fallen and injured were isolated along a fence and first aid crews, hastily organized, shouted for bandages and water.

A straining din of confused voices filled the air with an electric, almost palpable panic, and it is into the heart of this disorder that I was led.

Piling up around me were twisted and shredded bodies.

I stood still, watching a young man whose jaw was torn off

its hinge, struggle through his last convulsion. The medic attending him stood too, wiped his palms down his trousers and stepped over him to the next casualty, even before the young man's eyes rolled up in his head.

So this is it, it occurred to me then in a slowly crystallizing thought, at last, the collapse of Detroit.

The woman lying at my feet clutched my ankle. I set my instruments down beside her and set to work.

"How could I know? How did I know it was going to happen?" the woman whispered. "I knew."

I cut away her tattered blouse and trousers and discovered a gaping wound in her side and a dozen smaller wounds down her thigh to her knee.

"The air vibrated with restlessness for days and when I slept I dreamt a stream of ghosts flowed over me like water. Ragged scarecrows chewing the lips from their faces."

A large scrap of shrapnel and a bit of wire from a metal fence was embedded near her ribs. I tried to clip the arteries and sew closed her damaged organs.

"How could I know?" she said, "Because coffee burned my throat and the sky those last few days weighed on my shoulders driving me deeper into a region where I was just barely alive."

"The stores sold only cabbage and canned fruit and the butcher ran out of meat because the pigs and sheep in the slaughterhouse, rushing ahead of the catastrophe, died on their feet for no reason, and death poisoned their meat."

"The signs were there, I'm telling you."

"Even house people emerged from the shacks of rubble they'd lived in for years and walked the streets in plain daylight without covering their faces or shielding themselves from the air."

There didn't seem to be much point. She'd lost too much blood.

"My son breathed an anger so thick it damaged his brain. He paced up and down throwing over chairs, ranting and finally disgusted with the sight of his own face, he smashed a mirror and ran from the house. I followed, but was too slow and haven't seen him since."

I left her and moved on to others of the hundreds of injured around me. Torn limbs passed before me as on some grotesque

67

assembly line: Arms and legs broken when Detroit's buildings had suddenly exploded sending shards of glass and concrete flying. Cuts and bruises from falling down stairs or stumbling in the rush to escape. I labored with these injuries calmly because they were simple, mechanical failures of the human body. But I was not as calm when I began to realize there was something else here, too. It was the "epidemic" that had sent city officials to my door. It was not a disease, not catching, but, for lack of a clearer explanation, a sort of mass psychic failure among the refugees that in a short time transformed healthy men into whimpering idiots. The only identifiable symptom was the intensified language of its victims.

A young blond medic with hairy wrists waved me to his side. He shoved his pug-nosed face close to mine and said, "What the hell's wrong with this guy? He's weird."

He gestured to a mattress that was laid down on the gravel. The old man lying on it was thin and bent as sticks, his eyelids were almost totally swollen over his yellow eyes.

The medic's hand tightened on my sleeve as he leaned his large face into mine.

"Nobody brought him here. He just walked up to the ropes and said, Is this where I'm supposed to die? Only if you really want to, I said, and he shuffled around inside here, and now he's worse by the minute. I swear he was fine when he walked in."

When he paused, our faces were almost touching. I turned to the old man.

I swung my hand before his eyes, and pinched him with a needle, he did not respond. Not to me. But that is not to say he was still, because he silently pitched from side to side and flapped his thin arms in the air, opened and closed his mouth like a fish trying to cry out. His face alternated between a deep flush as blood suffused it, at which times he was swollen with energy, about to burst, his chest heaved as he lurched backward sucking air . . . and a deathly pallor that spread over his face and hands, when he would suddenly fall limp. I leaned over with my stethoscope, checking his heartbeat, and could not find one. From the narrow perspective of the merely physical, he was dead. The plumbing was broken. Nothing curious about that, and I prepared to move on to the next casualty, except that when I looked up into the dead man's face, I was startled to see his eyes still shifting in his head, his eyelids stretch open. He began to talk:

"It's not much of a life. It's not much. I'm sick of it. Bored. But it just keeps going on. Think it's easy being from Detroit with all them gutters filled with things that'll eat right through your shoes. It wears you out, and I'm glad it's gone. That place can fall down to Hell and it's not too soon. Let it go, I say, go away."

When he stopped talking, the old man began to live again. He was again filled with pain, his body thrown back and forth with an abundance of contained energy. Then he'd drop back dead:

"Lived in newspapers for years down there in the shadow of the Ambassador Bridge. Everybody knows nothing and walks around like they don't have heads. I'd make a noise and put matches in front of their eyes and they'd just blink. Every once in a while during a mud rain, one of them would crawl into my cellar, but I'd shove them out into it and watch them stand there not knowing what to do, pummeled with big gobs of mud, lost, and I'd laugh at them as they couldn't find their way back and they'd fall and the mud would heap up around them and they'd slide down into the low places and it'd cover them and I wouldn't see them again."

The old man's voice, brimming with hatred, survived a dozen deaths as I worked on him. When the body struggled back into life, his words stopped; pent-up inside, they strangled him. He thrashed around, gasping; his tongue a useless, uncoordinated thing, failed to untangle his speech. Exhausted, he'd fall back limp, passing over again into death, and his voice like blood from a stuck pig's throat, would pour out.

"See that foot, that twisted game foot. The sidewalk cracks open and I fall through to the under-tunnel where a pack of dogs with their appetites dripping from their mouths are waiting, and they chew hell out of my foot before I get it pulled up again. Detroit, goddammit, the place makes your head shake. Last winter the wind pushed me through a plate glass window. And besides that, I lost my hat."

Never in my career did I labor as intensely as I did then. Not because the old man's life or his breathing body or his pain meant anything to me, I labored because I did not want to hear him. It was too unnerving, too unearthly that this rag of an old man, dead, quite still on the mattress, addressed me, or addressed nothing, but flooded the air with words.

"Pigeons always circling the burning rubbish and the smoke, that black finger rising up to them. I know what they eat to keep alive because it's what I eat. Rocks catch in their necks and cinder."

The old man's voice continued behind me, a thin rattling thing like the buzzing of an insect, irritating. I looked around the school yard and could see that now there were others doing the thrashing dance I'd seen first in him. The younger ones seemed to have more strength to trap their words inside them and resisted the bursts of language, but even they succumbed to it, almost relieved, I think, when all the life could at last break out of them.

A colleague of many years approached. Normally a precisely dressed, fastidious gentleman, now Dr. Arends' disheveled hair was plastered to his forehead, he wore a mustache of sweat and his shirt was soaked and hanging out. "John, I don't know what's going on here," he said, "These sons-a-bitches won't die. Or I guess they do die, but they don't shut up. What do you do with something like this?"

A police sergeant dashing up, said, "Sir, we're starting to lose our civilian help... they won't stick around... I mean, look at this..." The man's eyebrows bobbed up and down uncontrollably.

I interrupted him. "You start pulling our people out of the crowd. Put them along the outside fence." With clear, simple orders in mind, he ran off.

Of course, the orders were useless. I didn't realize yet that since the whole city was filling with refugees, the 'outside fence' defined nothing. There was no longer any question of containing them.

"Listen, John," Arends continued, "We're getting more and more of these talking corpses. I tried drugs, the same ones you probably used and it revives them somewhat, but they fall back again. It's like they want to die, and everything they say sounds like a hundred years of bitterness."

The voices persisted around us, eerie, unsettling, unnerving. Police and firemen began organizing into teams of two and three and descending on the talking dead with blankets and pillows and rope, tying shrouds over their heads to muffle their speech. It somehow heightened the eerieness knowing that behind the swathed heads, the eyes shifted and blinked, the mouths worked up and down, the voices continued to expel scenes and fragments of Detroit. Others used bandages and tape to silence the dead refugees, and when they ran out of these, simply flipped mattresses over on top of them. We began to hear gunshots.

Of course, we doctors by now had no control over what was happening. There was not even the semblance of discipline. The mayor standing on top of an automobile hood, cupped hands over his mouth and shouted orders, pointed. No one paid any attention to him. Crowds of those who had come as spectators now hurried past on the sidewalks, muddling against those running in the other direction.

One of the refugees, in a trancelike walk, approached and when he was almost upon me, fell forward into my arms.

"Mice climbed out of the sofa and sauntered from under the kitchen shelves, sluggish, fat with sickness. They walked in circles, easily crushed with my shoe."

I let him drop to the ground.

"Telephone poles slanted over and wires, taut as bowstrings, snapped. The cement buckled and tore the porch off my building. I saw it. I saw it with my own eyes. And I knew what was happening."

By now almost all of the original refugees had slipped into this twilight death. Doctor Arends and I walked in circles among them, watching the transformations take place and listening as lifetimes spilled into the air around us.

The fall of Detroit. Life before the fall. The crushing weight of voices ...

Whole families still clutching each other, dead, babbling. Couples in limp death embrace. Again, the torrent of language. None of it frenetic or communicative in the least, just continuous, unremitting and unnerving.

That night perhaps two hundred thousand people crossed into the city. Dr. Arends and I walked together through the streets and saw every curb lined with them, the cars, the beds of trucks, the porches and alleyways, they were sprawled over the cobblestones in all sorts of impossible postures, talking madly. Few of our own citizens were still out, only a few desperate crews of men who were swathing corpses' heads, shooting them and one man who drove through them with a snowplow, scooping them into a loading dock at the back of a store. The city hummed with voices: The hysterical voices of the incoming refugees and the hollow voices of the dead. We saw the front door of a house open and a man and woman shove two bodies into the street.

We separated. I walked the remainder of the way home alone. My wife in the living room held my daughter on her lap. Both stared at me as I entered. I sat silently with them until dawn, unaware of drifting into sleep until I was awakened by a dream of refugees swarming out of the walls and enveloping me like some lethal gas.

I was greeted outside my door by an ashen face that pierced me with brilliant unblinking grey eyes. A young man with tousled hair and a pack on his back, draped over my mailbox. One of the Detroit dead.

"Nothing I could do about it," he said, "I was walking along the fence and I slipped and my arm caught on the barb at the top and so there I was hanging by the crook of my arm until I could lift myself up. I was seven years old and I still got the scar. That's what it was like in Detroit."

I pushed him away and he fell on the lawn mumbling face down in the grass.

Dozens of streets were simply impassable now with thousands of refugees littering them. In some sections they were stacked and leaning against each other where a group that had been walking, suddenly failed in a mass seizure, died and leaned over like some bizarre Greek chorus, motionless, talking.

The city was paralyzed as a million tons of dead Detroit meat fell upon us, and more refugees kept coming all the time.

Most of our citizens stayed at home, trusting to city officials to organize the clean-up. I'd see them with thin-lipped nervous looks lift the shades from their windows to peer at me as I walked past. I went to the city hospital where crews were being dispatched to designated areas to free main streets and emergency routes.

Workmen in the hospital parking lot stood around the back of a truck, laughing and drinking coffee together. A large cardboard box was on the gate of the truck. Inside it half a dozen or more heads of refugees were chattering as cogently as any that are still attached to bodies. It was rather like looking into a box of crabs, the jaws working up and down, the eyes still revolving in the heads. The men found some grotesque humor in this display.

In the hospital auditorium grim city officials, doctors and others gathered. Dr. Arends was standing along one of the walls.

"You missed something of a heated debate," he said, "They've been trying to decide if the refugees are really dead or not. The mayor wants them all shoved into ditches and covered over, or dumped in the river, anything to get them off the streets. But you know Golden, with his let's-talk-while-the-patient-expires attitude. He's been arguing quite sensibly, I think, that we can't really do anything with the refugees until we're sure that they won't come popping back to life and walk back where they came from."

"They're dead enough for me," I said, and told him about the scene in the parking lot.

"Well, that's just the point," said Arends, "Golden is arguing the absence of life signs isn't enough to justify doing away with bodies. No brain activity, we scanned a few of them this morning. No heartbeat, of course. No claret coarsing through the veins, but ..."

I nodded, "But being alive is usually a prerequisite of speech."

"Exactly. I haven't yet buried a patient that could still talk to me."

It was decided in short order with a dazzling show of pomp and indecision that we would continue to move the refugees to designated areas and decide from there what to do with them.

For the next two days, trucks moved through the streets loaded with bodies. The truck engines and the hollow sound of dead voices, that's all there was. Along the banks of the river we placed long rows of bodies side by side. All city parks, abandoned fields and vacant lots, all inessential roads were lined with them.

Besides trucks, automobiles with bodies stacked on their roofs, trunks and hoods crept through the narrow passages in the streets. Citizens heaped stretchers with three and four bodies. Wheelbarrows, even bicycles were used. Cars were packed and then nets of woven cable attached to their fenders and dragged. Hot air balloons and blimps scraping the houses on either side of the street, hovered a few feet off the pavement, yanking in their train pallets piled high. We were attempting to move hundreds of thousands of talking corpses through our streets.

At last the weather was the deciding factor. Because as we sweated and tugged with sheer brute force, the sun serenely shone down on the bodies, swelling and fattening them with legions of maggots and slugs and a thousand varieties of bacteria from the earth and air that opened wounds in the slowly rotting carcasses, so their fingers split and their stomachs exploded, even while their voices continued.

Their flesh rotted and the sun coaxed sickening lethal fumes from it that spread through every avenue, slid along every window and under every door, clinging to hallway walls, silent and deadly and inescapable. The smell of our sweat mingled with the nauseating pollution of the bodies.

Now it was obvious, too, our citizens were fleeing the city. Undoubtedly some had gone in the first day or two of the crisis, but now hundreds of our own people sought refuge elsewhere. Men suddenly stopped their trucks and left them idling in the road, covered with corpses, simply walked to their homes for their family and belongings and left. Our own population of refugees.

There were no longer arguments for preservation of the bodies in the unlikely event that they would spring back to life. They were obviously in too advanced a state of decay and the prospect of that flesh suddenly animating again was too horrific for argument. So the corpses were bulldozed into huge mounds and guardsmen with flamethrowers attached to their backs sprayed them. Citizens made small heaps on street corners and stood in rings around them, grim silhouettes through the night, as bonfires rose higher and higher. The streets blackened with smoke. As some of the refugees had been that first night, now our heads were swathed with rags to protect ourselves from the thick suffocating air. Our own voices were muffled against our faces and we communicated with gestures and worked desperately together trying to empty the streets.

It was strange, all those bodies talking as they were consumed in the pyres, but even as the ravenous flames caressed their flesh and peeled it, the monologues reeled on:

"Oh, no thanks, I said. I said, no doubt it would clog the

windshield wipers. Radioactive metals? Never mind them, I said, they make your eyebrows fall out. After all, I don't want my children going sterile ..."

Another grizzled refugee with smudged face pressed against that woman's cheek, said:

"Give the goddamn hand to the pigeon factory. It just wouldn't heal again after the birds got to it. So I took it off with a kitchen knife and threw it in the trash ..."

The flames tore apart their clothes, rushed to lick their fingers to smoke, and filled the whole sky with their weight. The mountains of bodies crumbled and fell down as if the ground opened beneath those charnel heaps and the speaking dead tumbled into some apocalyptic hole. We watched those massive piles disappear in the fire.

A thick membrane of smoke settled over Toledo blurring the edges of our own bodies, we were dim shadows laboring within it. There was no dawn that day as billows of darkness obscured the sun, and the sight of our own refugees leaving the city.

I could feel them, the rippling streams of people passing near at hand and hear their coughing, choking speech as they held on to one another fumbling to find the way out.

By mid-afternoon, the smoke was riding higher and beginning to lift. In the smoldering streets, ashes and bones in black mounds lined the curbs.

We were all soot-covered, sweat-stained and silent, as the wind picked its way over the tumbling ash. In pockets where it was trapped, by cellar steps, between buildings, in alleys, at brick deadends, it whirled in dry dusky circles. We tramped the scorched concrete ankle deep in the rubbish of incinerated refugees. We shoveled the remains into garbage trucks and scrubbed and hosed it into the sewers.

But it was a futile effort.

Though thousands of us had begun the effort to defeat the living dead bodies, our numbers dwindled as one after another of our shovels slipped from our hands and clattered to the pavement, and one after another of us, empty, and lost, walked away. A darker night than the one we'd just survived enveloped our spirits. Beyond panic now, beyond crisis, we had mingling in our bloodstream a despair, an emptiness that did not allow us even to grieve for our lost home place, our dry wasted city. We had failed, clearly, completely and finally.

The bodies were gone, it is true, but the voices remained.

There was no escaping the hollow voices that now swam disembodied through the air, washing this way and that with the wind.

They were undiminished by the loss of their physical bodies, in fact, they seemed enhanced, more penetrating than before.

A scratchy and uneven ghost voice spoke at my shoulder:

"You shoulda seen the electricity arc when it lifted my daughter off her feet in the hallway and tore her hair in seven pieces on the couch. I was tired of living in that dreary catacomb. I helped. I condemned Detroit. I unglued it."

Brushing a hand by my ear, I tried to flick it away, as I would a persistent fly. But the voice pursued me.

"It was too stale and naked and bitter. A desert in the shape of a city."

I moved further down the curb, trying to get away from it. Shoveled faster, bumped a woman who was poised, bent over her task, listening to a voice of her own. She stood up, we looked at each other, she clapped her hands over her ears.

"First a shower of glittering stones disgorged from the sky, exploded everything ..."

I dropped my shovel, began walking quickly down the street.

"Then the gravel and concrete hummed with a shattering resonance and crumbled so you walked up to your knees in dust."

In a sudden burst, I sprinted a block and managed to lose that voice, but picked up another.

"Detroit fell down," it said, "So fast I was glad. You wouldn't believe it, how that magnet of disgust sucked tea kettles and toasters through the air, hangers out of the closet, nail polish off fingers; bowls, spoons, glasses out of the cupboard, crashing through the windows out into that black fissure that opened in the middle of the street. I was so glad."

I now saw dozens of our people with their hands over their ears, walking purposefully away toward the city limit. A few however ran back and forth, uncontrollably confused by the voices and had to be grabbed, by shirt or belt by the purposeful ones and hauled along with them. Others sat still on porch steps or leaned against lamp posts, listening, as if hypnotized, but when we jostled or slapped them, they woke out of their trances

76

and joined the march.

My wife was upstairs in the bedroom, already packed when I got home. My daughter was asleep on the bed.

"We're leaving now," she said.

She wore a scarf over her mouth and there was a dark smudge on it where she drew her breath.

I nodded.

At the city limit, we left the voices behind. Looking back, the outline of our city, abandoned, soon empty of the living, still smoldered.

After a few weeks, my wife and I and other families attempted to salvage our belongings. We organized crews of deaf men who drove into town in trucks while we waited at the city limit. At the end of the day, the trucks came speeding out again, the deaf drivers waving their arms, grinning. The trucks were stacked from floor to ceiling with our most prized possessions. We were overjoyed until the truck gates swung open.

The voices jumped out at us from inside, having infested all our things like some dirty radioactive mildew.

We dumped it all back inside the city.

Somehow those voices had become infectious, because after our short exposure to them on the roadside, they whispered from within the clothes on our backs.

So, naked to the bone, we left Toledo that last time, forced by Detroit to begin our life again.

A Year of Kindness: *The Pigeon Factory*
(for Mick Vranich)

Our fathers were muscle and bone crafted by factories to fit machines. Their breath was a dark exhaust like tar that polluted the food on their plates. They were elaborate contraptions designed to fit into the space beside steel and the blades that trimmed it. Their names were Scrapballer, Hooker, Fork Driver and General Laborer. Their jobs exact and unforgiving: A misplaced finger was instantly sliced away and dropped in a slag heap where it wiggled like a question mark. They clomped down the sidewalk on wooden heels, drew keys from pockets with chrome claws. Our fathers were thumbless, jerry-rigged men. Irredeemably laborers. In the morning they left for work with black lunch buckets clamped beneath their arms.

Evening when my father returned, fibrous swellings of red, purple, green and yellow wire bulged from his pockets. His fingers were wire snippers, his brow furrowed deep as a hammer claw. He worked for the telephone company. What do you do there? I asked. "I make pigeons, for crissake." Really? A few days later, I tried to catch a pigeon, but it blurred into the air. Well, at least they fly, I thought, not as well as sparrows or crows, but for machine-made birds, clearly, the telephone company was doing a fine job.

Our fathers entered factories in droves, channeled between cyclone fences into passages so narrow their cigarettes burned holes in each other's pants. They entered those smouldering enclosures through clouds of air-borne sediment, guided only by dim bulbs hung on black cords. Hundreds of rods, wires and pipes knitted together over the men, an immense web that undulated with currents of electricity like fat strands of seaweed.

Sailing by on the Rouge overpass, we witnessed that vast sea of factory fed by a thousand rivers of railroad track, specks of shipwrecked men scrambled between islands of fuming steel. In the exhausted air, those desolate spots of flesh waved arms and shovels. From the freeway, they were smaller than ants on the sidewalk. A hundred of them wouldn't fill a thermos, a thousand of them could stand inside a lunch pail. How did our fathers get so small?

In my father's case, disease melted the skin from his bones. One winter his ribs abruptly jutted from his shirt, his shoulders folded around his chest until they came together beneath his chin. His wrists narrowed to parchment colored pencils. Only his hair seemed to fatten, blacken and thicken. At first we suspected softening of the will, a sludge of viscous despair; we thought an ordinary cancer gripped him and was turning his shoulders into a puny coat hanger. But when the roots of his hair changed to silver and maroon, turquoise and violet, it was clear the wire in his pockets infected him, that those hard worms of copper wrapped in bright jackets of insulation invaded the pores of his skin and were boring through his veins, metallic larvae flourished inside him. Then we understood, as spools of wire wrapped his heart, what manufacturing pigeons can do to a man.

He paced from room to room cursing his job. With clippers in one hand, he snipped the longest wires that looped around his head seeking another entry into him: A pore, an ear, a nostril. In the other hand, he wielded long-nose pliers, with which he drew out endless streams of copper filament. Terrible groans, barely restrained by clenched teeth, grated through the house as he ripped the wire out. For weeks he was a thrashing, suffering beast, involved in an agony that thrust us insignificantly to the farthest edge of his horizon. At last, one morning we discovered him on the living room floor in a bed of wire that was still wet with blood and sweat . . . collapsed, but breathing. He saw us looking at him. And the next day, he went back to work.

JOHN RICHARDS, writer. Son of the telephone company and a woman who sang so clear neighborhood children gathered under the window when she washed dishes.

RALPH NORRIS, painter/photographer. Born in the 40's to a car salesman and a waitress. Poland and South Carolina run in him. Mostly city runs in him.

NORRIS and RICHARDS live and work in Detroit. Always have and probably always will. May they rest in peace.

This first edition of *The Pigeon Factory* has been typeset in eleven point Mergenthaler Pilgrim at the West Coast Print Center. Printed and bound by Cushing-Malloy, Inc. for Cadmus Editions in November 1986. Composition by Wendy Shapiro.Design by Wendy Shapiro and Jeffrey Miller.